My 27duet

TWO BOOKS IN ONE VOLUME

A NOVEL AND SELECTED POEMS BY

Jean-Thomas Cullen

CLOCKTOWER BOOKS, SAN DIEGO

My 27duet

2 books in one ~ novel + poems

Contents

Note: Each book has its own Contents section.

Book 1: The Novel

Clocktower Books
San Diego, California
presents:

On
Saint Ronan Street

a novel by
Jean-Thomas Cullen

Contents

---

[1] Cymbalist Poems has its own table of contents.

"...and never lose the pebble to enchant..."

Companion volume to the novel On Saint Ronan Street

CYMBALIST POEMS

SELECTED POEMS BY
Jean-Thomas Cullen

CLOCKTOWER BOOKS, SAN DIEGO

In this *27duet*, forms Book II—Starts P. 169

Le Début au Fin

Chapter 1

A blue light came steeply from a clear, starry night sky to laugh with Jon Harney and Merile Doherty, who were making love in a down sleeping bag in the snow on someone's lawn—stealthily, among pine trees and cypress bushes around silent suburban homes—while unsuspecting folks slept all around them in West Haven, Connecticut.

Jon and Merile snuffled and giggled, writhing in each other's warm, sweaty arms and legs; rubbing feather-soft bellies together, and *ouch*, clacking knee caps.

He started to roll over on her but she pushed him back. Her hand brushed along his side as they wriggled inside a downy sleeping bag for two. "Stay a little while longer—I've never had so much fun."

He laughed and held her tightly as they lay side by side, looking out from their evergreen hideaway among white and sleeping houses.

A blue glow of streetlights stole with accessorial civility among the scotch pines. The air smelled sweet (scoured of its salts and sulfides, which lay buried). Sudden breezes runneled over the virgin snow fields, kicking up spiraling whitewater snow crystals, crossing the buried street to clip snow caps off dazed, beached cars. Jon and Merile sputtered and closed their eyes as cold grit blew freshly into their mouths, eyes, and nostrils.

"Whew. This is like riding in a fast motorboat," said Jon.

"Have you ever done it in a boat?" she whispered.

"No," he said truthfully, thinking of the nearby Long Island Sound and its Atlantic waters and its summers.

"You're lying," she accused, slapping his arm.

He lay back with his arms behind his head. "I wish."

"I haven't either," she confessed. He smiled, but she frowned and cuddled close, running her lips and hand over the hair on his chest. Between her cold fingertips, he felt the heat of her breath. She whispered barely audibly, "Let's not delay." They lay hidden in the shadows of pine trees.

He moved in between her long legs, guided by her eager hands; and, rocking on her firm round buttocks, consummated the release of deliciously hoarded energies. Crystal snow enveloped the hair at his neck as his head rose into tingling pine needles and they labored together. Their fingers were intertwined and white. Their groans sounded syncopated and in rapid counterpoint.

After they sank together in exhaustion, she stroked his hair slowly and steadily while he quashed a resting cheek against her shoulder. Sucking in his cheeks thoughtfully, he could see past the horizon of her cheekbone, chiseled and covered with microscopic hairs in bluish light. Her dark, liquid blue eyes, full of calculations, blinked as she looked upward through pine needles. Stars winked high up in the clear sky.

He murmured through a mouthful of inner cheek, "What are you thinking?"

She kept stroking his hair. "We're stark naked, you know that?"

In an exchange of startled looks, they burst out laughing—softly, of course—rolling about in a pummel and writhe of limbs.

"I'm getting chill," he said, burrowing deeper into the sleeping bag. With one long arm, he reached down past his fetally raised knees and icy toes. He sought his underpants among the clothing their trampling feet had compressed far down in the bottom of the sleeping bag.

She huddled down, too, while tightly zipping the mouth of the sleeping back around their brushing necks. "I suppose we'll catch our deaths. What are you reaching for?" She brought her knees up and aside, and added her hand to the search. Their fingertips scrabbled together over the pressed clothing.

"My underpants," he chattered.

"The primal fig leaf," she remarked sympathetically. To the changeless night she added, "This had to end."

"We could do it again," he muttered, knowing it was impossible. Finding the needed undergarment, he sat up and pulled its one large and two smaller apertures over his numb feet. In so doing, he let in a blast of cold air that raked their backs. With a subdued shriek, she flailed through their mingled clothes. "I'm putting on my shirt first," she chattered. Thus together they struggled to clothe themselves as quickly as possible.

He sneezed.

"See?" she said.

Their shoes came last; already their nylon ski parkas enclosed their body heats separately. The sleeping bag lay open and its newly exposed innards were becoming lightly fuzzed with blown snow.

With the heat of motion retained by the airtight parka, he hurried under the impeding pine branches to wrap the sleeping bag into a tight ball while she stood beside him, a figure of innocence. She kept her fingers linked over the opacity of blue parka and ski tag veiling her pleased secret. She remarked, "Say, we melted the snow in a circle."

Wheezing from icy air in his lungs, he swept the downy nylon hull under his arm, feeling it deflate slowly, and looked at the crushed, bare grass which was already covered by platelets of ice.

"Nobody would believe it," she observed.

He straightened up and looked at her. "Would you?"

In the blue light, her teeth were like china as she smiled. "I'm very happy." She was a tall, slim blonde with long smooth hair and an elegant sort of long-faced prettiness, ruddy and radiant as if just from the ski slopes.

He was dark-haired, lean, and muscular, with an angular, narrow head of short-clipped dark hair, a strong jaw covered with twice-a-day shadow, and mournful dark eyes.

"We made one mistake," he said, pointing to the scars their feet had made in the freshly fallen snow. The holes were already filled with snow, but had raised edges like moon craters filled with dust, mysterious in origin.

She shook her head. "It's going to snow some more very soon now." She put her hands in her parka pockets and looked around. "Suppose somebody was watching?"

He touched her elbow and drew her back into the shadows. "Come gaze into my eyes one last time."

"What about the footprints?"

He said, "If anyone comes by, we'll tell them it was a Yeti and we were chasing it."

"I have to get going in a few minutes," she said, staring worriedly at a foot of fresh snow already blanketing the street.

He shrugged. "We'll manage." He looked aside. "I think we've melted the snow in a circle around us."

Laughing brightly, she stuck a snowball down his shirt and he in genuine anguish made jerky motions like one who had been shot, falling finally face-first into the down.

Minutes later, he chased her over the glaciers of snow and ice that oozed from among somnolent houses. Disregarding man-made fences and barriers, Jon and Merile capered under tinkling and ice-laden trees while the moon shone gaily, trapped in the suffusive blue haze of the street lights. The night just sort of floated in a sympathy of winking stars as they held hands atop windy orchards and gazed toward the humming highway, near the sea; and toward the unknowable future for each of them.

Part One: Spring

Chapter 2

Jon Harney, alias Charles Egeny, was mowing the lawn one day around the Beechcroft Building, one of innumerable Yale University structures in New Haven done in ostentatious and timeless somewhat-Gothic.

The seasons in New England are extreme and final statements. It was spring—and talk about April showers. Gone were Chaucer's deep snows of February, and the agues of March. Like water dripping in a pot through tendered tea leaves, a gentle April rain sieved itself through the newly bright-green trees. The brown earth was soaked, and the first tender grass sprouted in thin, tall clumps over the tea-like deposits. The very air seemed to glow bright green, and was fragrant with emerging blossoms.

Far down along the concrete expanse of Whitney Avenue, high up over the banked tree crowns newly dense with fresh leaves, reared the damp red shafts of East Rock and Indian Head. The twin mountains were a tribute to the city, a statement of its small borders, an ultimate point beyond which the soul toiled to comprehend the goodness of the Divine giving anew each year this present of Spring.

Jon Harney stopped, turned off his evilly smoking lawnmower, and took off his rain-damp baseball cap to wipe off sweat.

He was twenty-three, and employed by the university in this manual capacity. Owing to his fledgling degree in English from a smaller, less well-known university, someone in the Yale employment offices had promised him this job as a starter, pending some more important and interesting assignment. Could he put up with the drudgery of mowing lawns for that long? Sure, he told them, what the hell—it was better than no job at all. Besides, having just finished his degree, he relished the thought of some relaxed summer time, innocently spent mowing lawns. He was tired from years of school, and not sure he wanted to continue in English. Through much of his undergraduate time he had faked it, reading few of the assigned materials, and writing (like running) for his life. He knew there were holes in his understanding of the standard Great Authors. He had preferred to read less well-known but more modern poets and writers of his choice—the cool jazz of writing, blue beats unknown in the bleach of academe; in whose tone and modality he wrote his own verse (free in more senses than one) that could connect with no safe, mediocre publisher. He hoped to have time, living in his rented room in Hamden not far from Lake Whitney—where, a hundred years earlier, the famed inventor had toiled in a small red factory that still stood there on an island amid moss-colored, marbled waters—to read all the authors and works he should have read for courses.

Meanwhile, he wrote poetry under the *nom de plume* of Charles Egeny. He'd published a few scattered items. Fame, however, was not yet at hand, and should it come, he would relegate it to the mysterious Charles Egeny, since he felt he should never succumb to some emboldening and inflated public image of himself. He preferred the freshness and early morning innocence of being forever an outsider; every day was thus a fresh beginning full of idealism and dreams. Confident in the eventual success of Charles Egeny, Jon Harney wiped his forehead and continued to mow Yale lawns with his blue-smoking lawn mower in the tinged and tea-dripping green half-light of a spring day in New Haven.

In the early mornings, a truck took the members of the lawn-mowing team around to their various work spots. Thus left to himself, Jon Harney took a craftsmanlike, artisan pride in conquering the upstart legions of newly sprouting grass. He had worked his way up a slope around the side of a building fronting on St. Ronan Street, and was just pausing to wipe sweat from under his cap.

Then and there, he saw Merile Doherty for the first time. Her footsteps, in half-heels, sounded muffled on the drenched and green-covered sidewalk above. Clad in a white dress that reached from her neck down to mid-thigh, she walked airily, innocently, in an elegant swish of slender limbs. She was blonde, and had that fresh, athletic, long face, blue eyes, and pink cheekbones of which advertisements are made. Her skin had a smooth, creamy tan like a flan pudding. She didn't notice him, and perhaps was indeed not conscious of being watched. For this reason, her walk and her facial expression were plain and unassuming, but to Jon Harney she was a goddess, and he frantically resumed his mowing.

Later, he went inside for a soda. Bending down in the wood-paneled darkness of the austere break room, to remove a cola he had just bought, he was startled by the whiteness of her dress as she came in.

"Oh, hi," she said. It was the obligatory greeting between people working for a long time in the same office building, who never get to know each other but eventually learn the contents of one another's clothes closets just from the daily variation among similar themes.

He backed away from the machine, removing the pop top from his cola can. She sidled past and inserted her quarter. He felt awkward, sweaty, and caught a whiff of some subtle perfume, some air of freshness about her.

Her coin slid easily down the innards of the machine, but her pressing of various buttons with a glossy fingernail produced no result. At last, seeing her blush of frustration, he excused himself. "Allow me…" Groaning with effort, he bent down on his knees, inserted a grubby hand into the machine's cool guts, and fished about until he felt a ledge high up in its intestines. On that ledge, his stretching fingers just barely touched the convex, crimped bottom edge of an aluminum can. "I have it now…" he gasped, and with a final effort (his shoulder being in the way) he freed the can and brought it down, balancing in a juggling act on his fingertips.

She smiled at his effort.

He rose, leaving the can for her. It lay in the slot where it should have fallen in the first place. They faced each other briefly before the machine. She was nestled up against the machine, her slender body hunched in a motion of preparing to retrieve the can, and her eyes darted full of pent-in sentiments from a glance at his dirty hands to the dully gleaming can and back to the muscles of his legs.

He stood transfixed as she bent close past him to seize the can. He inhaled deeply the scent of her fresh skin, the disintegration of perfume atoms in the warmth between her roused breasts. He stood back, soaking in the gentle but enveloping ambience of her faint smile. His breath—rattling with heartbeats—caught in his throat.

Around her eyes were the earliest of faint wrinkles, as if caused by the intense and mysterious and subtle melting effect of her smile. She must be about thirty, seven years past his own age.

Rising, she appeared startled by his attentive stare. She seemed utterly surprised, and then a bit cool and disenchanted by his hard, hungry look.

"Excuse me," he stammered, and the smile blossomed out again, crinkling the corners of her mouth and illuminating her skin pores.

They shared that dull, tea-green soaking glow in the gloomy basement room. Perhaps there is some springtime hormone that sets cells ablaze with new hope and yearning.

Their eyes met, engaged, and would not let loose. There arced between them a lightning of emotion. As she once said later, she could have turned away, and as he agreed, that would have been the end of it. He noticed the veiled, dull-faceted diamond, the glimmering platinum ring on her finger in that tea-soaked light—a green ambience flooding the dark wood-paneled basement room.

He yearned to reach out a fingertip and touch her cheek. She looked so open and glowing and helpless in that moment. But his fingers were grimy from the work outside and he hid his hands behind his back because of the proximity of her white dress. She later admitted she would have gone back to her office, where she had a heavy typing assignment. Instead, she sat in one of the billowy, plush old dark brown easy chairs in the lounge.

Jon Harney—fresh from combat with presumptuous spring grass fed by soaking rains—relinquished his battle and sank into the airy comfort of a parallel chair. She crossed her naked legs, pointing the toe of a white shoe at him. From the first, they laughed easily together. Every time their eyes met, there was that flash of empathy. She uncrossed her legs and modestly pointed her chiseled knees away.

"Do you mind the rain?" Her voice was plainly tremulous. Her lips quivered as she spoke. Her voice was high and exposed and uncertain, girlish and falsely devoid of strategy.

He knotted his hands around the cola can between his knees. Literary innuendo emerged. "Actually I'm enjoying myself. Every blade of grass is a challenge." He detected a quaver in his own voice. Had he been confronted with a canyon to jump across, his stomach pit could not have been more tense. He sat on the edge of the chair, ready to spring.

He thought, *What am I getting into?*

"I might enjoy escaping from the office too," she admitted, and in so saying conveyed a sense about her whole life. He sensed this and clutched the can more tightly, smiling nervously.

Her fingers fluttered, trembling, up around the watch she wore on a chain around her neck. "Almost time to go back," she said.

He looked at the floor, feeling a leaden weight of green light upon his back, and said sharply, "Stay a moment longer."

She feigned incredulousness. "Whatever for?"

He stared at the floor, noting the pale outline of her legs in the periphery of his vision. "Because I enjoy talking to you." Scared of what he'd said, he stared at her, and she sat back (imprisoned but willingly) by his look. She said: "You don't want to hurt me." It was a wish and a question.

"No, of course not," he said, swigging at the cola. "I saw you on the sidewalk before."

"I saw you too," she said.

There it is—door open.

He shook his head. "I didn't think so. You shocked me."

Her frown relaxed from worry into an intrigued smile. "Oh? How is that?" Still, her knees pointed away. She hadn't taken a single sip from her cola.

His truthful words, effortfully disgorged, ballooned leadenly around his head in the enclosed atmosphere. "I find you very beautiful."

At this her smile melted away into gratification, while her voice took on a mournful weight. "I don't look thirty and married, do I?"

"You sure don't," he told her. He was glad that her knees remained pointed away. "I would like to meet you." He had never spoken this way to a married woman before.

"A date?" she asked incredulously but not unkindly.

"If you want to call it that." He felt a panic rise inside. What about her husband? What about this job? What about...

She stretched her wrist so the cola can tilted in the direction of her gaze. She stared into the cola can. He watched her nervously as she deliberated. He almost wished he could run from the room.

She wriggled the cola can in her hand and regarded him thoughtfully. "You have nothing to do with Yale, do you? I mean, aside from your summer job or whatever?"

He shook his head.

She looked again at her cola can. "My husband is on the faculty. He's an assistant professor of archeology. We aren't doing too well. You aren't married, are you?"

He shook his head.

"Wouldn't help much to cry on your shoulder."

He started out of his chair, approached hers, and put his hand on her wrist, which rested on the armrest. "I'm afraid I only know about marriage in theory. I can't do much to help you." He'd only had one long-term girlfriend during his college years, along with a string of flirtations and a confetti storm of gratifications with young women.

She gave him an intense look, quickened by impulse. "You don't just mow lawns, do you?" she said, alluding to his humble occupation.

He told her his secret, "Under the name of Charles Egeny, supposedly a Russian émigré, I write poetry. Fits the void left by Nabokov."

She put down her cola and put her hand on his. "You'll make it someday."

He talked jive, "I read the Beats and the Audens. I compose word-o-fone like Coltrane or Stan Jets play sax."

Does she get who I am? What Charles Egeny does?

"You play with language," she said appreciatively. She was thirty but looked younger. The long, elegant cast of her cultured face betrayed a lifetime's pursuit of social directions, including tennis courts, cocktail parties, and lawn club debuts—in short, of the wealthy.

"I type my manuscripts at night," he confessed while moving intimately to kneel by her chair, lithe as a panther.

She reached out and absently stroked his hair. "You'll have your success," she said encouragingly. He saw, in her look, a habit of being (in his disdainful view) associated with intelligent and aggressive but weak men. He held back, proudly, when he saw men like her husband. They were shadows of conformity; weak in their all-consuming need for recognition. Such powerful arrogant and sweaty men filled her world. He radiated his refusal to be like them—now or ever.

"I don't need success!" he protested, rising. "I don't care about recognition. All I want to do is write poetry. I want to mow lawns, conquer grass—and find someone like you to adore."

Upon this confession she regarded him with confusion and admiration.

I would write poetry about you in adoration.

They bent their faces close together, and their lips brushed. It was the electric connection they both needed at that moment. He pulled away breathlessly from her moist, cool, soft lips. The directioning of her chiseled knees was in disarray. One pointed to him, the other to the slatted narrow basement window. He noted the cool pliancy of a pale inner thigh, momentarily exposed.

She reached out to touch his hair.

She rushed from that undersea cavern.

He wiped his hands on a paper towel, and slowly got ready to return to his blue smoking mower in the soaking green light outside.

Chapter 3

They sat by a rainy, runnely window in the rear room of George and Harry's Restaurant on Wall Street. It was Sunday. Dribbles drummed on lead gutters outside. The narrow street, framed by high neo-Gothic Yale buildings, glimmered in a greenish half-light. From the music school near the restaurant issued complex but neutral piano studies. Some anonymous person was pensive and dreaming over the keyboard. Tentative notes complemented ivied walls and drowning spring blossoms crushed in a film of water covering the street, while more water dribbled obscenely out of high eaves and splattered along rust-stained walls.

Jon Harney felt embarrassed. All week long he had yearned and schemed toward this meeting. Now she sat near him and he had nothing to say. She sat with her back to the window. Her hands were in the pockets of her open raincoat. Her blue-jean clad legs extended on sharp high heels under the table. Her head tilted expectantly while her blonde hair hung down into the windowsill behind the bench back. He sat askew in a corner, one finger in the mouth of the beer bottle he'd finished. It was an ale bottle, brown as amber, in which light glowered amid slowly falling foam resembling rain—or sea water. He alternately studied the worn mouth of the bottle and the white buttons spaced in a generous arc on her blue shirt.

"I didn't know if you'd come," she said. Her eyes flicked toward the ceiling beams full of worry and determination.

He leaned forward and soccered the bottle between the palms of his hands. "I was afraid you might not come."

I was afraid I might not come.

She sat tensely but let him move close so he inhaled the essences of her hair, her skin, even her tea breath. His eyes fell to the soft salient which pushed her shirt way out, and what quivered underneath. He was surprised to see her sharp breaths, her trembling breasts.

Her finger felt icy with fear when he touched her hands. They were not those of a young girl. If she were a charcoal drawing, he could have washed her to a glowing blur and she would have passed for the essence of a very equestrian, sapphire twenty-three (his age) or even a preppy, pristine seventeen. Hinted rilles and dry cross-etchings were as yet only a preliminary design—over her knuckles, at the corners of her mouth, near the orbits of her eyes.

Seeing his look she did not protest. "You don't always."

"Always what?"

"Older women."

He shoved the bottle away. "My own age and younger."

"Oh. So far."

"I guess." The wrinkles could be from too much sun if she'd tanned too much over the years. She was the type for skiing, sailing, tennis, slender cigarettes if any, and credit cards, all prescribed for Ivy League; none of which he had. "You don't feel older." He corrected, "Seem."

Getting ahead of ourselves. The signal is still red, but the signs ahead are clear to read.

She looked directly in his eyes for the first time. Her eyes were frank and grateful. "You seem like a wise rebel."

"It's relative," he concluded.

"I had nobody to feel older than," she said. "Bill's thirty-four. Sometimes. Or sixty-four. Or four. Depending."

"Bill." Thinking of this other man made a sweat burn inside his collar.

I wish you wouldn't talk about him.

Seeing his look, she pursed her lips and studied the flotsam of lemon seeds and tea shreds in the brown lake at the bottom of her cup, aground on a sand bar of stained sugar. "I won't say anything again. After all, it's not your problem."

"Does he beat you?"

Her glance was sudden and bright blue. "Oh no. No, no. Dear."
She laughed out loud. "I would be lucky if he gave me that much
attention." Her teeth were unflawed white. "You needn't worry. He's
gone to Australia. They're digging near Upskate or something on the
North Coast."

"Sounds interesting."

"Doesn't it."

"If you happen to be in Upskate at the time."

"I'm actually rather Downskate."

"And here we are."

"There you are." She reached for her pocketbook. "That's about
the way it is." She touched his arm. "I'll be back in a moment."

He sat alone, listening to water gurgling gently in secretive
drains. Clocks moved slower in this oceanic time, where massive
waves of leaves made a rushing in your ears, and your heart beat too
hard and too fast. He knew he was free to get up and leave. Silly
though—run? From what? Morality? No, a single transgression could
not be very expensive. He would be mowing other lawns in this
garden of easiness. Charles Egeny should savor forbidden apples and
write firmer beats.

He heard her footsteps in the hollow wooden room and turned to
watch her approach. She could easily be twenty or twenty-one. She
smiled as she approached, guilelessly. Hands in raincoat, steps sure
and direct, chin up…he thought he had the answer.

She hasn't been domesticated.

Still wild and coltish, she slid in along the bench, quick to be
beside him again. He reached impulsively and put his hand on hers.
She laid her other hand on his. Their bones and skins were dry but
mortised together in a sensuous tension. In planetary gravity, they
were the architecture of circumstance: skillfully engineered canals
laced through intricate chambers of cartilage, muscle, and flesh.

She might be complex, but she was not deep. She inclined her
head slightly away and gave him a questioning look—a friendly but
pained contraction about the mouth and eyes. "What are you
thinking?"

*We are accomplices now—spies or assassins—or at least thieves
in the night, a well-matched pair who can telegraph each other's
brain waves; fight or flight.*

He took her hands in his.

She let him hold her hands resting on the table, her fingers pliably relaxed but unhelpful.

"You're not troubled by existential questions?"

She made the faintest motion of shaking her head.

No such logo at the varsity tennis shop.

Her teeth were still white but the smile was gone, replaced by distance and indifference. She said, "Are we going to discuss what is reality?"

We're in an East Egg roadster, doing ninety in a forty zone with the top down and our hair flying behind us.

He released her hands and put his hands in his lap. "I was hoping we wouldn't."

She gave him a long, beautiful, sexy look. Her eyes darkened, and her wide, glossy lips took on a deeper shade of Merlot, with a smart, cutting laugh. Or was that Harlot? She wrapped her arm through his and pulled him close to her firm, warm side.

"We aren't going to, are we?"

"What?" She looked at him mockingly.

Talk about why the sky is blue and stuff.

She shook her head and said in a throaty voice, "Nothing complicated."

He said ruefully, "You are more experienced."

You have money. Or, Bill has money and he has you. Or—he has the bills, and you have Bill, rich bitch.

She brought her hands together and made a gun of them, aimed at his heart. "I enjoyed what you said back in the break room on St. Ronan Street."

"What did I say?"

Devilment glinted in her eyes. "About needing success. What a declaration! All I want is to write poetry. I want to mow lawns, conquer grass..."

"And love women like yourself," he finished. He rescued some fervor out of his momentary uncertainty, "What else could a man say, looking at you?"

"A man," she said, making a fist of her fight hand on the table and reaching with her left to grasp his knee and squeeze under the table. "That's how I like you." She squeezed his knee, shaking it with surprising intensity, and leaned close and said with tea-breath, "I'd like to take you by your grass…and mow you!"

He felt relieved, and they both laughed.

Some bubble had broken, a tension had disintegrated and filtered away in pieces into this greenish air.

"What I want," he said, "is to be honest and open. I have this feeling we can have that."

"Maybe Charles Egeny will write me a poem."

"He did last night," Jon Harney confessed. "He fell asleep though before he could retype it."

"Honest and open. Those qualities are hard to find, unless two people hate each other."

"What I mean is, I have this feeling we don't have to act, know what I mean? We don't have to play games."

"Does it bother you I'm married?"

"You bring me neatly from the general to the particular. Yes."

"Would you love me and leave me, excuse my cliché?"

"Maybe if it was the right thing, or the right time."

She raked the opposite wall, the fireplace, the stained glass windowlets, with a gaze filled with hot and cold computations. "Maybe that's how it should be." She darted a look at him. "Suppose I don't surrender?"

He spread his hands in the air. "I would dip my colors to you in salute, and pass you at a respectful distance."

She placed her hands in her lap. "Would you think badly of me if I…had you on board?"

"I'd bring my best manners. Charles Egeny would rhapsodize you in the third person."

She was resigned to her sensibility. Lying back again with her hands in her pockets, she looked up at the ceiling. "I wouldn't get you get into anything embarrassing, or dangerous. Bill won't be back for three months."

"Why doesn't he have you along?"

"He asked me. He asks me every time. I just don't want to. Things won't be any better in Australia."

"Upskate."

"Downskate."

"Cheapskate," he said, knowing it was the last thing about the world in which she sailed.

"Ice skate," she said, signaling with her eyes. "Make me warm, Charles Egeny. Warm me up, Jon Harney."

He took her hands in his, and rubbed them for warmth. "Love is free."

She laughed. "That's a hippie thing."

"We're not at Woodstock."

"I'd go anywhere with you."

In a play world, we could orbit the earth or be in a yellow submarine blowing bubbles at smiley fish.

She shuddered. "You make me feel warm and loved."

"You don't have any kids either."

"We tried. Half dozen years ago, when we were first married. One of us can't. Bill has a really low sperm count. Jeez, why am I telling you this? Because you asked, I suppose. Don't get a headache over it."

He felt lost. "Have you thought about a divorce?"

My freedom means everything to me.

"We've talked about it. Then Bill runs off quickly on another dig."

"Are you satisfied with being alone all the time?"

"Yes, in a way. I can do what I want. Not going out, I mean. There is always something to do. I'm not answerable to anyone. I see Bill off on the plane with a feeling of relief. When I drove him to the airport last month, I could sense he feels the same way. So the feeling is mutual. And what's marriage except mutuality? Maybe we have a good marriage."

"By that logic, I suppose."

I will never understand.

"Do you ever feel like a prisoner?"

She arched her eyebrows ironically. "I've never known anything else. That's why I cherish your wild freedom."

"I thought I was just poor, and horny."

She tickled his ribs. "And creative."

He put an arm around her. He could feel her vertebrae like tender, submissive, vulnerable steps to her soul. He wanted to possess her, and have her, and pour himself into her, and hear her laugh, or listen to her surf-like breathing as she gently snored beside him, full of dreams like the sea.

She spoke at the ceiling beams. "I like the idea of being married. I'm not sure about actually living it day to day. When I meet a stranger I enjoy saying I'm married. I enjoy seeing the envy. I'm attractive to men, who mistake that as meaning I'm happily married, whatever that means to them. They look closely, trying to read the truth in my hair, in my hands, in my eyebrows. Don't get me wrong, I don't toy with anyone. I just like to leave them on that note. It's like credit, like protection." She gave him a sudden, violent look. "I have never screwed around with anyone."

"Is this screwing around?"

Ready to walk.

She took his hands in hers, as if to blow on them and heal the sting. "No, baby. I don't know what this is. Maybe it's friendship. God knows I am so alone it scares me."

I hope you don't own a gun.

"You're worried about me." She made a reassuring face. "I won't do anything to hurt myself. I love life too much." She added, "The last thing I want is to hurt you."

He pushed his hands out and wrapped them around hers. "I am not looking for anything hurtful. This is like science."

She laughed. "What?"

"Gravity. Mutual attraction. The moon and the earth. The earth and the sun."

She stroked his wrist slowly and considerately, as if reading his fortune. "Maybe you can shed some light on me."

"We can help each other. Not that I'm in much need."

"Me neither. Or maybe we are and don't know it."

"You're nice to look at," he said. "More nice to sit with, look in your eyes, watch how your lips gleam in this rainy light, and love the warmth in your soul."

She pulled herself close as if they were high school kids on a date. "We can split a banana some time."

He laughed. "A banana split."

"Splat." Her eyes glittered and she looked *gamine.*

He knotted his hands together on the table, squeezing her yielding hand close to his chest. "Why you have this thing about you, something young? At twenty feet distance you could pass for twenty-one. You're like"(he groped for words, diplomatically)"not yet domesticated. A girl."

"A girl, always young." She looked grateful. "I'm still filled with impulse."

"Yes."

"I am careful, though."

"Are you sure nobody from the faculty would recognize you here? I mean, after all, we're at the center of the university."

"In a restaurant? Some university—I'm sorry. Like there are spies everywhere."

"You can be a little cynical."

Biting, maybe, which gives you a cutting edge.

"I'm sorry. Sometimes I get to be a wise guy, a wise ass chick. No, I doubt if anyone would recognize me. Bill takes me to parties and shows me off. I don't really mind. Are you shocked? I was brought up that way."

"You told me you are from Westport."

"That doesn't mean I'm spoiled. My daddy is a famous surgeon. My older brother is an architect. Groomed for Harvard, so naturally he went to MIT."

"And you?"

"Do you know the Style commercial?"

"You mean that new cigarette." He remembered the ads—always anchored on a smiling, tanned blonde accepting a Style from some curly-haired rascal holding a crisp new red-and-white, candy-striped pack of The Really Thin Cigarillos.

"It's a cigar," she corrected. "I was groomed to smile and hold the cigar. Like Momma. She held the cigar for years. It was the only thing she could train me for. So I hold the cigar for Bill when he needs me. My face and a few cocktails too many got the chair in anthro somewhere on the West Coast to invite Bill to teach for a year. Bill turned it down for Yale. But he's in Upskate, and here we are."

"Here we are," Jon said. "How did you get the name?"

"You mean Merile?"

He nodded. "I'm Jonathan, the prophet from the Bible."

"No," she said ironically, "you are Jonah who was swallowed by a whale."

"But he escaped and got barfed up on shore."

"Lucky you. Well, my parents couldn't imagine me as a finished product for the Seven Sisters and some Ivy League cigar smoker unless I had a name right out of a commercial. You know, a soap opera name. So they named me Merrill. Which is so masculine that it's almost like there is no woman in the starched blue shirt, just a concept from an ad for expensive whatevers. So I changed it, in the still of the night, all by myself, playing around with the dial until I got it more supple and moist like a girl's handle should be."

He made a dreamy face. "Merile does sound feminine and mysterious. Soft and mushy."

She laughed. "It's so subversive. You say it the same way— *Merrill*—like a suburb in Cos Cob, or a hunting rifle in Africa, or a tragic regiment in Flanders; but it's really like a Parisian mist, or a Belgian waffle, or a Yalie donut."

"I like the donut part," he said. *Keep the Yalie.* "My father sells cars and my mother bakes a helluva cake. My older brother's in the Army. My younger brother James is studying Political Science. I'm the first person in the history of my family to finish college. I mow lawns for a living."

"Do your parents live near here?"

"In West Haven," he told her. "Jimmy's the big hope in the family. He was president of his class in high school and he wants to go into politics."

She regarded him minutely, running a speculative tongue tip around inside her lips. "We grew up not far from each other."

He thought for a moment. "I was starting high school when you graduated from—where was it?"

"Vassar."

"Vassar, of course."

She posed with raised shoulders, a cocked head, and batty eyelashes while making airy motions with a fluid hand. "Vassar...o to dream of holding your cigar!"

"You don't have to hold any cigars for me."

She slapped his wrist lightly. "Of course, you ain't got one. Being from West Haven and all."

Mildly annoyed, he peered at her in the watery light.

"I don't think that way. Please don't be annoyed. A lot of girls in my class at Vassar went off to hold their own cigars. It just so happened I wasn't endowed with the sense of independence. My role is more to the hearth. I spin and Bill goes delving. That whole bag, you know?"

"You keep the fires banked?"

"That's coarse."

"And to the point."

"I get the point." She sighed. "Penelope, spinning and chaste by the hearth in Ithaca." She crossed her arms, wrapping her elbows in opposite hands. "If I didn't feel so...affectionate...about you I'd be insulted."

He rubbed his stomach. "It's getting late and my stomach tells me it's time for supper."

"What do you usually do for supper?" she asked.

"Burger Barn," he told her candidly.

She irradiated him with one of those warm smiles he'd come to love. "I could go for a Quick Yack." The verbal ping pong was over. The net was discarded, the table folded; they walked out into glowering twilight and drizzle arm in arm like two twenty-three-year-olds—her blonde hair flying, his shoulders spread proudly like a sailor's.

Behind them, bottles made chinking noises. Piano music welled up from the Venetioid windows of the music school. Dribbles drabbled as they huddled, dashing. Envious looks followed their departure into the dripping and fresh spring and mossy evening. He knew she knew he knew now what it was like to have a woman like her holding your cigar. Not such a bad feeling; like being intoxicated with all that Fairfield County money and fire and first-class Scotch. Those smiles, like thrown snowballs. That skin like sweet caramel wanting to be licked.

Better yet, remove the wrapper and stare, but don't spoil by touching.

With her, he felt the anything, the indulgence, the experience at last of life. Somewhere sat her dark gray Porsche or whatever it was, locked and sullen and mysterious. Jon took Merile to his old blue Pontiac. Rather than mind, she seemed excited by it.

Chapter 4

B aa Baa Baa Baa Baaaaa, Barbra AAAAAAnnnn..." Jon and Merile sang. The radio in his Pontiac blared oldies but goodies.

Merile stretched slowly and deliciously in the passenger seat beside him. Her crook'd arms made brackets above her head, while her palms nearly touched the fluttering rag ceiling of the dark blue car. Her eyes were half-closed and her lips widened in a shuddering sense of satisfaction. The windshield wipers throbbed in rhythm with the music beat. The wipers' back and forth arcs scattered emerald buds and vegetal granules to the edges of the windshield. Her coat fell open, revealing a blue shirt budding with promise.

He felt entirely right, having her at his side like this. "Let's play Teeny and the Boppers," he suggested.

"Hokay," she yawned, then suddenly unyawned with a wet-dog shake of the head. She curled up to rest her head on his leg. Her arms stole around his waist. Her fingers stole nervously over his skin, fluttering here and there in little electric motions testing the muscles of his peritoneum. It was the first time she'd put both arms around him. He hadn't done that to her yet.

Newly spring-greened trees loomed on either side of the road. The windshield wipers thudded rhythmically against the chrome molding of the windshield. Spatters of water glanced before his eyes, filled with refracted light. He glanced down. A spill of blonde hair filled his lap. Her raincoat half-covered her long legs in a sprawl under the dashboard.

"Good Good Good GOOOOOOD Vahbrahtions!" the radio crackled.

The familiar local disc jockey burbled, "In case you haven't guessed it, tonight's California night and we have for you the Beach Boys and surfers in a solid hour of oldies but goodies not so moldy and pretty darn goldy and if you're told you're old just grab a hold, be bold, hang ten and you'll be sold…"

"I'll fold," Merile said with a laugh.

"Anything but cold," he said.

The Pontiac's tires hummed amid tea-like deposits of new blossoms. The car rolled into the wet brightness radiant around the Burger Barn near the Hamden Mart.

Merile sat sensibly upright, combing out her long hair, a couple of hair pins clamped in her lips and eyes wide as she sought to adjust her hair in the reflections inside the windshield. She turned the rearview mirror to point at herself.

* * * *

They stood side by side in the hamburger joint near the beach in West Haven. Merile chewed a wad of bubble gum pink as her tongue. Her lipstick was now candy-apple red.

Her arm linked into his, and her hip pressed against his hip. He didn't need to force it. She was giving herself to him if he would take her. He took her by the waist and pulled her close, claiming her. Her waist was slender, her figure fluid, her skin sinuous in his hand.

Animal love. Give me everything.

She whispered in his ear, "Our first date. Oh god you drive me crazy. I want you."

He pulled her close, filled with wonder at how her body molded into any shape he needed her to assume to please him, and she could not give him enough of her gyrations. Good vibrations. He had a rod on, torch flaming at the muzzle already. No woman had made him feel this way in years or ever.

The cash register rattled and chained continuously, and blue-aproned figures darted about behind the plate glass, scooping French fries, bagging burgers, tapping colas, squirreling out spiral deposits of

ice cream. White paper hats rode jauntily askew over teenage
eyebrows.

...First gear I'M ALRIGHT, second gear UPTIGHT, third gear,
HANG   ON   TIGHT,   faster,   faster,   faster,
FAAAASSSTTTEEEERRRR... echoed a timeless carollade by the
Beach Boys—or was it the Hondells?

Spring air was mild. Rain had stopped. The line moved slowly.
Children bawled. A ruddy pot-bellied duck pin bowler in a red nylon
jacket stared at Merile. A tall, skinny high school boy with spider legs
and pimply face arced high to drop-shoot a plastic bag of trash into a
ditzy dumpster.

"Plebeian," Jon murmured into her blonde hair, which smelled of
bubble gum and shampoo and car exhaust and Parisian perfume in the
lively nocturnal air.

She avidly chewed. "Aw, not much different from Westport.
What's missing is the air of everyone being hipper than everyone
else." She blew a bubble, and popped it with a smacking sound.
"Maybe even hipper than hip."

"Hipper about what?"

"The big cigar, of course," she said. She rolled her eyes up and
smacked her gum loudly. The tip of her tongue flicked out to lick
pink off of her lips. He silenced her gnashing with his mouth. She
succumbed breathlessly; their teeth touched. Their lips worked
frantically and savoringly together.

"Hey up front!" cried a beardless face possessed of a paper hat,
pimples, and sarcastic mouth.

"Lots of onions!" Jon cried, disentangling himself.

"Please," Merile said.

"Skip the onions," Jon amended, bending to be heard through the
aperture over the counter.

"No onions," echoed the boy, slapping a cardboard tray bull of
bulging, drippy white baglets on the counter. "A buck ninety."

"Hu, hu, hu," laughed the man with the red jacket and beer belly,
yellowishly devouring a mustard sandwich (or something Plebeian)
nearby. He raked Merile with dirty, greasy onion eyes like the skin on
a cheap hot dog.

Merile clung to Jon as he paid.

"Hu Hu Hu yourself," Jon said, spiriting Merile and the
cardboard tray back to the car.

"IF EVERYBODY HAD AN OCEAN…" the parking lot resounded.

Air smelled of rain, blossoms, motor oil, beef, ketchup.

Souped-up cars roared nearby, and the air had a sharp, intoxicating tinge of ether—almost a surgical ethyl breath.

Jon closed the car door, trapping Merile in an amber of his life, whose stagnant atmosphere was tinged with neglected upholstery, old newspapers, and unwashed clothing amid ghostly shadows. She didn't seem to mind.

They turned the radio down low. Merile fussed daintily with the waxy paper wrappers on her lap. Jon munched hungrily on a Yack. "I could be Vito. You could be Donnalee. Your mouth looks like a piano."

She was just raising a hamburger with both hands. Her teeth enclosed the hamburger, tearing an edge off. "Daf Fnark 'n Foo," she corrected, reminding him of Westport nomenclature. There was a soap opera about Clark and Sue, and an entire community of raptors who seemed to do nothing but screw each other—the men the women literally and viscerally; the men and men, or women and women, figuratively and sadistically while dollar bills twirled in air.

"Efcufe me," he said, dabbing some French fries in ketchup. "Forry, hummot fum Wefpoht. Umfum Weft Haphen. We haph no fidarf here."

She nudged him with her elbow, rollicking with puffed cheeks and spread mouth as she happily mauled her meal and the beach boys sang SURFERRRR GURRRRLLLL…

Later she curled up against his side in the car. They were parked outside her apartment on Everitt Street, about six blocks from St. Ronan Street. Realtors and ads in New Haven still described such buildings by how many Victorian worker families they held in a previous century, maybe a dozen persons per unit; today, the high-ceilinged antiques made for vast, echoing two-person apartments.

"You nife," she aped with an empty mouth—no gum, no burger, no cigar.

"I fink I'm fo-fo," he gimmicked. In the still, fresh night air, the hood of the car kept banging and pinging in a cooling-off music. Ignition keys hung under the dashboard.

"I fink fo too," she said. "How about some tea?"

"I guess," he said.

Car doors slammed in the evening stillness. He followed her lurching heels up a wind-flickering, honey-lit concrete path under weeping willow trees.

Call them weeping widow trees.

Her keys rattled, and soon the door stood open— colorful stained glass panels in a sturdy oak frame.

"I'm on the second floor," she whispered. She put her finger over her lips for him to be quiet. "It's what they used to call a four-family house. Now it's four Yalie apartments where maybe four dozen working people used to live in Victorian times."

He tiptoed behind her up a creaking, carpeted stairway. He longed to touch that rocking rear, those shapely legs, and the rest of her. He wanted to undress her slowly, enjoying her enjoying every moment of his attentions. It would be a matter of minutes now. He watched her head toward him as in a spinning, unavoidable slow-motion crash on a snowy winter street; both drivers are helpless and see each other coming, bracing silently for impact, dreading injury, and calculating fender repair costs.

On a shadowy second-story landing, she fumbled with more keys. The smell of her hair and skin drove away a musty carpet odor. Someone had a cat. The rain-dribbled window crawled with plant shadows. A door creaked, a shaft of light fell out, her sharp heels pounded over polished wood floors. Quickly she kicked her shoes off. For the first time that day she was shorter than he. She swung the door shut. "Here we are. Make yourself at home. I'll get some tea water boiling."

He was on his own. It was a spacious apartment. The doorway led into a small vestibule crowded with coats and umbrellas. A door led to a bathroom, another door to the bedroom, another door to the kitchen. Beyond the kitchen, Jon found himself in the living room. Plants hung from the ceilings, a poster glowered in black and white on the wall, low and fluffy furniture glowered in the light from the kitchen. Books, a stereo, posters, plants, a chandelier, scattered rugs, a pile of record albums, a casually flung nylon stocking, his first impression. Multiple identical windows in a row looked black and curtainless, dappled with raindrops. A clockwork encased in brass chimed. It was ten o'clock.

"Don't turn on any more lights," Merile said.

"You haven't needed curtains," he commented.

She regarded the black windows, "No, not until now."

You've been a modest girl, but that could change.

He sat on a black leather ottoman and brushed the stereo with his fingertips.

"How do you like your tea?" she asked.

He turned. Sitting before the stereo, he could reach out and touch her ankles. Which he did, feeling nylon over skin and bone.

She sank down and embraced him on the shaggy rug.

He kissed her while his hand explored the exact shape of her. He started to touch a button on her shirt.

She pulled away. "I'd better turn off the tea water and shut off the kitchen light."

She was tall, walking into the halo of kitchen light while he lay on the thick carpet while the other man's stereo glowed, and he pressed the off-switch.

Her shoes clattered on the hardwood floors until she kicked them off. Her footfalls were as quiet and pattersome on bare planks as raindrops outside.

The lights out, he heard the swish of clothes being removed. *When a woman has long legs it takes longer for her to remove her underclothes*—so he guessed.

She pattered on bare feet, closer. He watched her figure undulate in gloom for him.

"Do you like me?" she asked, echoing her own unanswered question about tea.

"Turn around slowly," he said.

Silvery moonlight burnished the glossy wood floor. Her pale figure, singed with a bluish light from street light strained by budding tree branches, turned in a white archway.

She turned slowly on long, naked legs and the moonlight was egg-pale on oval buttocks, round breasts, her smile…

Chapter 5

He awoke because a sunbeam dazzled the orbits of his eyes, because a hand brushed against his shoulder, because a droplet fell on his bare chest. He opened his eyes and sat up but she had left the room in a rustle of skirts. "I have breakfast for you," she said in the kitchen. The apartment was endowed with the aroma of coffee, the essence of a light perfume, the stirring of a fresh breeze from some half-open window amid the stale odors of sleep.

Twisting aside to get out of the direct sunlight, he remembered that he must get off to work. He buried his head in the pillow. Bird twitter and consciousness that it was Monday made him swing upright into a sitting position. He awoke fully when his soles touched the cool wood floor and he heard the crackling of bacon in a pan.

The bedroom where he had intruded and borrowed time and love was a study in white. The house was undoubtedly very old, one of those rambling, turreted wood structures built in New Haven during the last century and remodeled every generation for transient use by faculty or business families.

He saw the source of the breeze. While he was asleep, Merile had slightly opened a glass-paned door leading to a wood porch palisaded with flower boxes. White and red blossoms stirred in sun and wind. A delivery truck hummed through the quiet street outside; cowboyed to an impatient stop at the corner with crashing contents.

A broad picture window overlooked the porch. Yellow curtains hung pinned back by heavy brocade cord, revealing banked and newly green elm trees outside. Jon Harney rose, belching, and staggered, stretching and rubbing his head, yawning, past a wall covered in books (rousing creative jazz in Charles Egeny)—into the living room.

His clothes were neatly folded and stacked on an armrest of the couch. Daylight filtered in through a sea of tree crowns outside, in a rich and golden stream through a three-sided bay window overlooking a long, narrow backyard. Cross-streams of light from the bedroom and a window at the side of the house stirred millions of dust molecules dancing in a faint breeze. The days of sifting spring tea were over, he thought, sitting beside his clothes. Soon, spring rains would turn into drifting clouds of gray humidity. Colorful pleasure boat sails would criss-cross Long Island Sound.

Merile poked her hand and face around the doorway in which she'd twirled nakedly the night before. "Do you want to take a shower?"

He looked at her and nodded. It was then he learned something about her. Her long, elegant face fluttered with a white smile. Her cheekbones glistened and a tear fell from her chin. "You'll have to make it quick because I still have to finish drying my hair," she told him.

Puzzled, he gingerly entered the kitchen.

She handed him a towel but turned away. "Hurry, your eggs will be ready in five or ten minutes."

He would normally have steamed up the bathroom, but he did not want to cloud the mirror.

Anyway, it was spring, finally, and he half-opened the window and stepped shivering into the cold tub behind plastic curtains fragrant with hundreds of past shampoos. He showered quickly, lathering himself, his hair, then rinsing away the sweat and sticky dried sediment of the night's exploration. He marveled that a person could smile and cry both at the same time.

What is it about you?

"Your eggs and bacon are ready," she said, opening but not closing the door and then fumbling in the sink.

"I'll be right out." He turned off the water and dried himself behind the shower curtains.

It was a small, ancient bathroom with tall ceiling, tiled walls, and separate sink spigots for hot and cold. Its milky-rippled window set in warped wood were rarely opened. She bent over, washing her face, as he sidled past wrapped in his damp towel. It was 7:15.

"I'll drive you to work if you'd like," he said.

She groped blindly for a towel. "No, thanks. I'd rather walk. Thanks anyway."

Not to be seen. Not to have betrayed yourself. Or Bill.

Jon stood awkwardly as she dried her face and smiled at him with gleaming red cheeks.

I have never met this guy but I'm calling him Bill.

Her eyes radiated a glimmer of shame. He reached out to embrace her. She came a bit stiffly but unresistant into his arms.

"I slept well," he said.

She pushed gently. Her brief glance told him she had not slept well. Her eyes glistened. "Your eggs are getting cold."

Your eggs too.

He ate silently, and had to swallow every mouthful with difficulty. He relished only the electrically perked coffee which was aromatic, strong, and yet delicate.

Like her precious bush.

She hurried from the bathroom with her hair in a turban and a bath towel wrapped around her slender body.

"You could be in commercials, Merile."

"Oh please, sweetie." She came close and pecked him on the cheek. "You know how to flatter a girl."

"Merrill," he said, and she understood.

"I'm all about the cigar. I know. I can't escape."

She dressed quickly, bouncing with hurried motions on the living room couch. She emerged from the bedroom, restored to that formal, *gamine*, almost wounded, sultry prettiness as he'd first seen her. A delicately flowered skirt reached from her neck to her knees. High heels made the calf muscles of her long legs tense in an accentuated stalkiness. Her carefully trimmed blonde mane bounced about her shoulders and forehead as if she were trapped in a TV commercial landscape without time or cares.

She sat down beside him as he tied his shoelaces. She folded her hands in her lap. She had drawn fine mascara lines through the pale hairs on her eyelids. The mascara on both lower eyelids was faintly smudged.

She asked, "Do you have everything you need?" It was a preamble to saying goodbye.

He did not want to say anything glib, noting that could be mistaken for bluster or flattery. "I'm very content, and a little guilty," he said.

She nodded, staring down into her tightly welded hands. "I am too." She said quickly, "Look, I want to say thanks. It was swell, yesterday, the Beach Boys."

"It was fun," he agreed.

She laughed directly. "Guilt sort of adds spice."

He finished tying his shoes and folded his hands between his knees. "I wasn't looking for the guilt part. I supposed I deserve it."

She leaned over, folding her arms so her elbows rested on her thighs. "It was a long time coming. It's my fault, I'm sorry."

He said, "How can you laugh and cry at the same time."

She fumbled for a tissue. "Talent. I'm kind of silly."

He laid his hand on her leg. "Do I cause that?"

She shook her head, dabbing her eyes.

He rose, feeling sweat break out at the back of his collar. "Look, Merile. Can we sort of…just treasure what happened? Can we sort of…say it was swell?"

She grinned. "I realize now that I really want you to love and leave. Go on, Lothario. Split, will you?" she nudged him. "Abandon ship."

He stared at the telephone by the couch—a mistake, he suspected dimly then, and would later realize.

She put her hands on his shoulder and kissed him briefly but warmly behind the ear, a friendship gesture.

"Go, Charles Egeny, split. Write something in remembrance of me. A lovely silly and ultimately pointless poem in which you charge around in your Pontiac with flags flying and Beach Boys playing…"

He turned away. "Should Charles Egeny write that you were in distress? Did you hang your hair from the window? Did he slip in the ivy and sprain his ankle? Was there a pointlessness clause contractual and in writing? And what, pray, was the essence of this dragon you say you heard sneaking around the house, dear lady?"

"Let's say the lady was undecided about the rescue."

He tried to take her in his arms. She wriggled away. She smiled broadly. "Time ran out and the lady was still clueless. The call for help was premature. Charles Egeny rode off vowing to help— whenever, if ever, requested."

Jon made a wry face, feeling pained. He remembered, "Charles Egeny had a pressing commitment which caused him to ride away without helping the lady. It was a prior commitment not to become committed."

At the door she framed his cheeks between her hands and said, "Charles Egeny helped the lady very, very much by his mild manner and…oh, go will you? You'll be late for work."

He bounded down the stairs, into the green blossoming of true spring, unburdened, freed from the sudden tangle.

Putting the top down, he rode off hurriedly into the sunshine and stray dew droplets. The last tea leaves were gathered around street drains, waiting to be swept from their gravel and asphalt beaches down into the pipes and ultimately the sea.

Part Two: Summer

A telephone waited by a couch. Once a week, a duster held in long, slender fingers descended to brush away the effluvium of time, that weightless dust of motes, some of them raining to earth out of the sum and essence of spent meteorites, others rasped off mountain tops by the wind and after airborne months seeking shelter behind white and remodeled walls; some, more prosaic, raised out of the pores of the sun-baked sidewalks of New Haven, pressed through the old walls after a brief flight to tumble microscopically over the fields of wood and rug and couch. Sometimes the stereo glowed in dusty warmth with throbbing music. More usually it was quiet, a silence filled with the rustle of cellulose crackling in growing house plants, the rustle of a stray breeze in yellow curtains, the padding of bare feet on sticky wood floors, the sigh of a comb through long blonde hair, and once in a great while, the murmur of a voice speaking alone. From the gardens below, ghostly children's voices rose when sunlight flooded the room, echoing generation after timeless generation in their playful conflicts and conspiracies.

It had been a hot, sunny day and now night steeped the room with inky-blue-black promise. The telephone slept, cut off by the weight of its receiver from the million-fold electronic babble washing the city in conversations. A fan hummed, oscillating under a rubber palm on a teak table. A gadzillion of crispy leaves crinkled directly outside. It was the earliest summer heat. That rare, brief moment of year was at hand when one would be comfortable with the temperature of evening, when inside and outside falsely promised never again to be irreconcilable, when moths brushed blindly against window screens, when a lemon ice could pierce the palate with citric relief, when streetlights outside were yellow and friendly.

A distant and electric urge startled the sleeping telephone, but did not yet cause it to ring.

The apartment was bathed in a cool blue light. The dry, warm voice of a TV announcer, the rustle of thousands of baseball fans, the stirring march of a razor blade manufacturer made the dim apartment come alive. A pair of long, slender pale legs were draped carelessly over the armrests of an easy chair. Long fingers crunched in a bag of popcorn. The air smelled of salt and butter. Ice tinkled in a cola glass. A taxi tooted outside. The phone rang. A jet whistled high up in the night sky amid thinly banked clouds under some constellation. The phone burred under the rubber palm. The taxi tooted impatiently. The phone burred. A car passed in the night. A door slammed in the rambling, turreted house.

"Hello?"

"Merile?"

"Yes?"

"Jon Harney." A car door closed, a taxi radio crackled, a motor revved, tires rustled on the dry street speeding away.

"How are you?"

"I'm okay," he said.

"How are you?" she repeated senselessly, feeling an unexpected surge in her stomach.

"Okay, how are you?" he insisted.

She dropped an uneaten handful of popcorn into its bag and settled on the couch, her long bare legs shimmering in the TV light as the million fans shouted, a bat cracked, and the leaves crinkled outside, bringing in a fresh and sweet-smelling breeze. "I didn't think I'd hear from you again," she said.

"Maybe you were right," he said.

"Where are you?" She heard the unmistakable sound of a tractor-trailer rig passing on a busy street, and realized not quite immediately that it wasn't outside but on his end. How close they were, so far yet in one head together like a pair of earphones, a left and a right, a male and a female.

He sounded bored. "Oh, one of these bars. A regular meat rack. I want to leave."

"It's ten o'clock," she told him.

"I hope I'm not calling too late."

She rolled over on her stomach. "It's not too late." Her breath somehow was short.

It's never too late. I'm always open for you.

"Just thought I'd call," he said.

"It's been a while," she said. She added teasingly, "What about your date?"

"No date," he protested.

"It's Friday night," she said. "A date night."

"It's springtime too," he reminded her.

"I know!" she agreed, accentuating the "know." Her fingers were somehow aflutter around the receiver.

Fig night. Fog night, she thought. *Come over here.*

His voice sounded abashed and sweaty. "I'd made up my mind not to call you."

She laughed incriminatingly. "I thought I saw you staring at the telephone when you were here."

"You don't miss much."

"You were standing too close. You must learn to be discreet."

"I thought I was discreet."

"Not discreet enough." Her heart was pounding and the pulse in her throat threatened to cut off her voice. Indeed, her throat tightened, so she involuntarily emitted a faint cry of desire. Embarrassed, she hoped he didn't notice.

"Instead I'm concrete," he said.

She pressed her elbows together, as her nipples tingled just hearing his voice. "I thought you'd be off mowing other lawns."

"I was," he said truthfully.

"Don't sound so enthused," she said.

"The grass is greener on the other side."

"That's original."

"I miss you."

"I know," she said full of sorrow and hope, yearning and soap. "Stop some time."

Come now. Please, I need you so much.

Crack! another home run. The fans rustled in Shea Stadium, and the announcer said, "With the bases loaded, Sammy Krakow drives a second home run for the Mets in this spring evening home game…"

"Someone there?" Jon Harney asked.

"Not a soul," she said brightly. "I got a card from Bill today. They found some bones."

"Over in Australia?"

"Where else?"

"Upskate."

"You remembered. Yeah, Downskate."

"I hope I'm not bothering you."

"I was hoping you'd call. Don't drop the receiver in shock now."

"You are so saucy."

"You could talk too long on the telephone."

"I can hang up."

"No don't."

"Shall I drop by?"

"What about your commitment?"

"What commitment?"

"To remain uncommitted."

He paused amid grass and crickets and exhaust fumes. Feigning casualness, he said, "You're on my way home."

"Do you like popcorn? Do you follow baseball?"

"How are the Mets doing?"

"Six aught," she said, feeling a warmth creeping into her stomach as she ran a toying fingernail over the crushed velvet material of the couch's arm rest.

"Sounds like an interesting game."

"If you like I'll make some more popcorn."

He said, "I'm crossing the Rubicon as we speak."

She hung up and went into the bedroom. In the stillness and darkness there, she found some silk briefs into which she slipped her long legs. After a brief deliberation, she decided to leave her breasts bare, and pulled on a mid-thigh summer dress. In the mingled light of moon and street lights, she turned slowly before the bedroom mirror and regarded herself. She would act nonchalant at the door.

Or, anyway, I'll try my best not to seem eager.

In the mild cross-lights, the puckering of her nipples in the flimsy flowered cotton shift did not show at all, but it made a magic glowing lantern to entice him with her figure.

The telephone glowered righteously under its palm tree. She stepped into high-heeled open pumps which accentuated the length of her legs.

"The die is cast," she said to the telephone, breezing past the TV to make some more popcorn.

"The bases are loaded again and this looks like a take-away game, folks," said the TV.

"De dice is trone," she intimated airily to the mute black telephone.

Minutes later, as popping sounds ensued from the kitchen, she stood behind the window overlooking Everitt Street. She'd had curtains installed—like a fig leaf, a sort of an expulsion from Eden theme—and pulled them apart for a peek. Any moment now a dusty Pontiac would come careening around the corner. She heard the sound of a car engine revving not far away. She raised her eyes, gripping the window sill with sweaty hands.

What am I doing?

His sleek Pontiac, top down, crawled around the corner. With fluttering hands, she let the curtain fall shut.

Chapter 7

On a day not longer after, on Everitt Street, trees glowed brightly and the buds on the trees were even brighter golden-green as Jon Harney and Merile Doherty sat on the porch outside her bedroom sipping iced tea and lazily regarding Saturday morning tree tops.

"This looks like a day to drive somewhere," he said.

She sat back contentedly, hands folded in her lap, a restful smile turning her cheeks solar. "What did you have in mind?"

He lifted the tea glass and studied its fresh sediment in the morning sunlight. In some spirit of mutuality they had invented this small gesture, They shared a glass. They drank from this glass in turns, refilling it often from a plastic pitcher full of clacking ice cubes. "Where would you like to go?" he asked.

She pursed her lips and arched her back. Her bare ankles wriggled on the porch palisade. The late June breeze ruffled her fine yellow hair. "When was the last time you were in Vermont?"

He shrugged in some embarrassment. "I haven't been to Vermont in five years. I've only been there once, with a ski group from college. I can only imagine Vermont full of snow. Why? How long of a ride do you suppose it is?"

She sat back, giving him a sedate and reasonable look. "Too long, I'm afraid. It would take us a few hours."

"We could spend the weekend!" he enthused.

She shook her head. "I keep thinking Bill might call. Somehow I wouldn't feel right about taking off for the whole weekend, not without writing him first."

Jon Harney set the glass down, careful to avoid any show of jealousy. What right did he have? He'd resolved not to question her commitments. Somehow he always returned with a faint bitter taste to these reminders that their relationship was bounded, that there were limits. A thunder clap, a landing 747, a few bones from Australia, and he'd run. She was the only thing keeping him contented with his lawns and flower gardens. He wondered if he'd have quit by now—perhaps find some coat-and-tie job or maybe bury himself a few more years at some graduate school, only to end up mowing more lawns because he had no inkling of the practical now nor would he then. Sadly, the Bills of the world were born with this kind of street savvy. They had this boardroom, mahogany-row deep pile carpet smell in their blood from birth. Jon Harney, first in his family to rise above trucking or mucking, had cruised into the sky but was lost, flying blindly in dense cumulus clouds of poetry and sincerity.

Merile bit her lower lip speculatively and looked at him. "I have a week's vacation I can take this summer. That's nine days, if you count weekends. If you want, maybe I and my imaginary girlfriend Mimi could take a week's ride up into northern New England."

He frowned, more for her than himself.

She held out her hand for him. "You care about me, don't you?"

He took her hand in his. "I love you."

"No."

"What else could this be? Am I sick?"

She smiled. "That's Shakespeare. This is reality. Jon, I love you too, like a—"

"—Husband?"

"Like a lover. You are my lover. I am your—"

"Wife?"

"Silly man. I am your girl, your dream, your whore, your bitch, anything you want me to be."

He fought conflicting feelings, to leave, to love, just not to like. It was more than that now.

She pawed at him. "What do you want, Jon?"

I want you to love me like I love you.

She read the look in his eyes and stared. "You should leave if you are going to hurt yourself." She reconsidered the legalese in that look. "I don't want to hurt you." Then she made faces as if seeing him for the first time. "Oh, baby. I do love you. I am just—stuck like this. A beetle trapped in amber. You are a poet, Charles Egeny, free as the wind. I am a prisoner, and you brought me a loaf of bread with a file baked in it, but I am too weak and foolish to saw my way out or even see my way out. What would I do? I keep busy typing and filing, a little light reception work. I couldn't possibly support myself." She paused. "I never finished college. I wanted to take singing lessons, but I can't hold a tune. I was going to major in communications, but I can't write. I was going to be a history major, but I can't remember the difference between Julius Caesar and Caesar Salad." She stroked him as if he were a pet chinchilla. "Baby."

"You are beautiful," he said. "You have a doctorate in being perfect. I am a shmoe who mows lawns. I know, one day I'll teach English or something. I don't even want to think about it."

She laid her head on his lap, the girl from the cigarillo ad, whose husband was that craggy handsome cowboy riding away into orange mesas in the remote provinces of Upskate and Downskate. She would never age nor want for money nor fail to speak in symbols (Ivy League, Seven Sisters, Lah-di-Dah).

You are not leaving Bill to run away with me.

He rose, took her hand in his, and sat on the armrest by her legs. She breathed in deeply, a gesture of sadness, "Jon, this trip to Vermont might be the only few days we ever have together. I mean real days together, where we can be alone and without any thought of being seen or being wondered about." With the corner of her eye she indicated the dense tree crowns all around. "I'm pretty sure nobody can see us, and even if they do, they don't know Bill, and nobody would wonder about you being here…" As she spoke, her eyes evinced a deep and sincere thirst to drink from his cup. Their age difference was, after all, slight. She looked younger, and he could pass for older. He bent his head to kiss her hand. He half-lifted her willing, elegant paw, but stopped—instead, more gallantly, he lowered his crown to honor her.

"Okay, maybe Vermont is too far. Maybe there is someplace around here where we can have a picnic," she pressed.

He rose and lifted their communal tea glass. The liquid tasted sweet and bitter. Her hand fell onto the thin cotton of her dress, and he noted its early, faint patterning amid the late-hour tennis tan. She saw her hands too, and said, "It's just a question of those few days. You don't have to think there's a trap. Only what's in your head."

He looked doubtfully out into the tree crowns, where a darting squirrel zigged and zagged evasion patterns across warped dark-gray bark.

Jon took Merile not to Vermont but to Sleeping Giant Park, a half-hour drive out of New Haven toward the north along Route 10. Traffic was heavy, and the heat set in, so he put the top of the car up. He wore blue jeans, crew socks, loafers, a hang-ten shirt. She wore white deck shoes, pink socks, and a simple skirt of light blue denim. A halter top freed her long caramel arms and slender hands.

"I keep wishing you weren't married," he said along the way, regarding a stubborn red light with frustration.

She budged slightly in her relaxed position, legs extended under the dashboard, one hand in her lap while she watched her other hand toying idly around the mirror outside the car. "I'm older than you. The age difference would bother you soon enough."

He shrugged, shifting gears and slowly releasing the clutch as the light turned green and summer holiday traffic edged along.

"Ultimately it will," she prophesied. "That's why it doesn't matter that I'm married."

Puzzled, he glanced at her; then concentrated on the road ahead. Suddenly he wished he were far away, tipping beer or chasing girls with one of his male friends. A feeling of futility overcame him, making his hands doubly sweaty.

She smiled wanly. "I supposed one day Bill will find the right bones and come back to settle down with me and spend a lifetime writing important papers about his discoveries. Maybe that's the reason I stay put like I do. We're okay together when he's here."

Jon said in a sickly voice, "Please…"

She sidled across the seat and laid her hand gently on his thigh. "I'm sorry. I was just thinking out loud." She reached up and stroked his hair. "I want us to have a good time today. Don't be sad or angry."

He gritted his teeth, full of frustration and futility. What was he doing getting himself emotionally involved with a married woman?

She sat close to him and said softly, so close that he could feel the warmth of her breath in his ear and inside his collar, "You wouldn't marry me or anything. I know Charles Egeny, maybe better than you think. I know you're not about to tie yourself down, but I also know you're in the back of your mind always searching for that perfect young girl who is going to make you happy."

He pulled his ear and collar away. Tears threatened to blind him. He actually heard himself sob, as if he were someone else.

She however pressed—"Please listen. I know how you feel about me. I feel it too. We are crazy about each other. But it's unrealistic to suppose anything is going to come of our relationship. Even if I were to divorce Bill, I really don't believe you would marry me. I don't believe you would tie yourself to me. And I know it frustrates you to feel your emotions going down a dead end. But it doesn't have to be a dead end. Maybe just a…brief stop. You can spare me a few hours here and there can't you? I won't stand in your way."

He laughed and brushed the wetness from his eyes. "I suppose you're right. What would I do now, anyway? Drive around? Drink beer? Buddy up with my old friends and talk about how we'd like to get laid if only we found some ripe young chicks or maybe…"

"…Maybe pick ripe fruit from the married tree?"

He nodded. "I guess that's sort of what I'd be doing." He sat upright and put his hand on her knee. "You're right. This feels like— say, remember that night, with the Beach Boys?" A hard rock tune resounded in the dashboard speaker, and abruptly the mood was broken as they rolled along happily making pretend.

"We're just on a date," she said.

We're just kids playing house.

"Yes, and I haven't dared yet to touch your boobs."

"No, you haven't even gotten as far as to put your arm around my waist."

"I'm going to try it, you know."

"I see that look in your eyes. I'll fight you off with a chair and a whip, you lion."

"I may be a lion, but you are a pussy."

It's fun to pretend, to play, to fight like this.

"I am open for business anytime you want to get your whip wet."

"I'm ready to pull over and take you right here."

"I wish we could. Too bad you don't have a van. We could make love in the back and nobody would see us."

"I'm going to love you in the back, in the front, in the bush."

"You make me all wet when you talk dirty to me."

I will never find another woman like you in my life.

As he drove, she gently massaged the back of his neck. "I cried about us."

"What?"

"We are a tragedy, baby."

This really hurts—but it's such a love-hurt.

"Oh god now I am getting all wet again—in the eyes."

"Don't, sweetheart." She nuzzled his ear, nibbled his lobe, snuggled her cheek against his shoulder. "My poor baby."

And I am so wet for you.

He bit his lip, put his arm around her back, and drove along as life must be driven, one stoplight at a time, staying with the flow.

She stroked his chest with feather-light fingertips. "I will never forget you and you will never forget me. I love you, Jon Harney, Charles Egeny, free spirit. You will always remember me, because that is our fate. Neither of us can help who we are or where we are or what we are."

Fucking Bill. If you were a man, you'd be here in this car, driving this beautiful angel, telling her how much you love her. It would be you in tears over her, not me.

"I love you very much," he said.

She did not answer, except for a faint squeal buried in his chest. He looked down to see the gold of her hair, to smell warm salt water as if they were floating in a summer sea. The heat of her tears soaked his chest as her head rocked on him with quiet sobbing. She didn't mean for him to hear, but he heard her anyway, keening like a lost child, over and over again, that broken wailing sound. Her hand lay curled helplessly on his thigh, upturned away from him, grasping for the impossible or just for mercy.

* * * *

They made a stop to get gasoline. They went to separate bathrooms and washed their faces.

A while later, feeling empty and in love and in the moment and strangely composed (as in the eye of a storm), he turned the corner into Sleeping Giant Park. On the right were the white buildings, sharp spire and manicured acreage of Quinnipiac College. On their left reared the trees and slopes of the Sleeping Giant Mountain, which you could see for miles around, looking truly (if you squinted slightly) like some gigantic Indian, hooked nose and all, arms folded on his chest, dozing away through the ages sunken deep into a bed of tree crowns.

I've only known her a few weeks; I may never see her again. She's a fox, she's available, she's hungry—a rare combination these days. Summer is here and the beaches are loaded with bikinis.

The park was full of people. Merile sat glued to him, with one arm over his shoulder, and her other hand on his thigh. Her body pressed against his at every possible spot. This short time was theirs and she was his. Nothing else mattered.

"Looks awfully crowded," she said, peering past the back of his head at the picnic area filled with cars and people in Bermudas. The cool, dark woodsy air was filled with char smoke and the sounds of barking dogs and squalling children.

Driving on, he said, "Too bad. There is a nice pond near there with a waterfall."

"Probably crowded to the waterline," she said.

"Maybe we should drive a little further," he said.

"Feel free," she intimated.

For some time the car crawled on a winding and tree-crowned road.

"How's this?" he said, pulling into a secluded nook between great shady trees.

They stood outside the car and stared uphill into wilderness. His hand sought hers, and her fingers eagerly entwined with his.

He speculated, craning his neck. "Wonder what's on top of that hill?"

She pretended a pout of protest, lifting the hem of her dress. "I didn't think we'd be mountain climbing today."

He shrugged and stared at the back of the car, where the cooler and picnic basket were stored and ready.

"Leave the cooler here." Hungry for something else, she nudged him. "Come on, we'll find privacy up there someplace." She started up the pathless hillside. He followed her. The climb immediately drew perspiration. The grade quickly grew steep, and she clambered with tennis court agility up over the huge mossy boulders, around mushroom-infested tree trunks, hand-over-hand up fields of sprawling exposed roots, sweating through short bright leafy fronds, careful not to let any twigs whip back and hit him.

He followed, at times scrambling on his hands and knees, but unmindful of the bruises and an occasional mosquito bite. He had eyes only for her long legs, her pertly rounded behind, her churning muscular thighs and the bunching of her underpants between struggling buttocks and legs.

Their circuitous route took them upward several hundred feet, mostly on reddish sandy stone, and whipped by punishing saplings. The Pontiac disappeared from view behind and beneath them. For a few moments they saw only tree crowns. The only human sound was that of an airplane distantly circling for a landing at Tweed-New Haven airport on Long Island Sound. In the bright sunshine, they broke through tangled underbrush and waist-high reeds. "There are houses," she pointed accusingly into the distance, and he winced at the sight of gray and white rooftops slumbering under the trees.

We wanted to be alone, he thought, wishing he could give her that, but even such a simple wish was beyond his reach. *I could never provide for her.*

"Come on, this way," he said. He made for a dense growth of pine to their right. They plunged through tall grass, suddenly downward into the cool darkness under the sweeping pine boughs. The underbrush was sparser here away from the sunshine. They clambered downhill around huge tumbled boulders left by the last great ice age, for the North American glaciers had stopped growing precisely here and then melted, up to two miles deep and full of boulders and other debris. The ice had melted, receding toward the north, leaving its load of boulders behind. Early Puritan mythology claimed the boulders had been thrown at each other by good and fallen angels during a war in heaven. The area had place names like Sodom, Gomorrha, and Satan's Corner.

"Oh look!" Merile gasped, as if staring at a miracle.

They stood between high walls of pine and gray, split rock, looking over an expanse about thirty feet in diameter and oval shaped. A shallow pond of still and moss-green water lay with mirror surface on a depression worn by eons on the rock shelf. Water from high rocks, fed from the highest land, trickled in a steady waist-thick stream down into the edges of the pool. The smooth stone around the pool was covered with old leaves and blooming moss in thick patches.

"I wonder if anyone knows about this place?" she said.

He shook his head. "I've never heard of it."

"Maybe it is a mirage," she ventured.

"More likely it's a well-kept secret of the people living near here. Look." He pointed to a cache of empty beer cans tucked under a rock ledge. The cans were filled with tobacco-brown rainwater and had been there for some time.

"We should have brought our picnic along," she said.

"Do you think I'm going to climb down to get it?" he said watching her sit down, take off her shoe, and shake twigs and dirt out.

She squinted in the half-light between the pines and the tall stones. "I wonder if anyone will blunder up here."

"We'll hear them coming for a mile." He walked in fascination around the rock pool. Water dribbled loudly down into the edge of the wide pond. Green surface scum pushed away by dropping water maintained a thick pressing circle around the waterfall.

"It trickles away through a split in the rocks at this other end," he told her, watching the overflow gurgle away. His voice must have carried with a faint echo, because he was surprised at the loudness of her voice, "I wonder where all that water comes from."

He pointed uphill. "All those beer-drinkers peeing up there…"

"Ve-ery fun-nee!"

He nestled down on his side and elbow beside her. "This could be our little hideaway."

"Until the owners of those beer cans return," she said, finished tying her shoelaces and sitting with her arms wrapped around her knees.

"Merile?"

"Ummh?"

"What you said back there. About us, I mean. It's true."

"I know," she said, glancing at him briefly, then continuing her study of the tree tops and sky.

He looked in the same direction, squinting in the sunlight and chewing on a grass blade. "I'm not trying to use you."

She shook her head. "I know that." She paused. "What dopes you men are, with your fifteen-pound egos inside three-ounce brains."

"What do you mean?"

She grinned and rubbed her hand along his neck. "I didn't mean anything nasty. It's just…well, did it ever occur to you I might be using you?"

He shrugged. "It occurred to me in one way or another." The panic from before threatened inside again.

She lay down on her side and elbow facing him. "Silly, we're both using each other. So what? People always use each other. It's not always malicious. People need each other."

He looked out over the still pond. "Why do I feel this desire for you? It's like fire. You know what scares me? That I may not be able to control it."

"That scares me too sometimes. Not being able to walk away smiling."

"You at least seem to be able to laugh and cry at the same time."

"Not an easy trick for me," she said, undoing her bracelet. "This is from a ritzy store in Manhattan," she said, throwing it. Green slime absorbed it without a splash as it sank, a golden, twirling treasure in clear water underneath.

"Why did you do that?"

She crawled close on her elbows and wrapped her hands around his shoulders. "Something of us together has to stay someplace deep inside."

He took her hands, squeezing them between his, and she gently reclined on the mossy stone under him. "I don't understand. Every pore of your skin makes me dizzy. Why is it when I don't have any right to you that I feel I could squeeze you close and never let you go?"

She smiled, her blue eyes sparking in the mossy half-light. The laugh welling up from her diaphragm was a husky, mature one. "Do you think I don't feel the same way? But would you let me own you?"

He made a wry face. Inside, though, he thought, *You already own me, Merile. My woman. My girl. My love. My sweet pussy. My eternity.*

She read only what she wanted to perceive. "See? It's that we're living in fire but we're ultimately not a threat—a danger, maybe, but not a threat—to each other. There aren't any strings attached." She grasped the hairs peering over his shirt top and pulled him close. "I could devour you. I could hold you in the palms of my hands like a butterfly. But eventually I know I'll have to let you go. Did you ever have a pet like that?"

He rolled back laughing. "You're sending me back farther than I'd suspected. I've loved and lost but...oh God, who knows, maybe once a long time ago I think it was an ant farm, and the neighbor came home weaving drunkenly in his car and ran over it where I'd left it in the driveway. I never looked him in the eye again. I was heartbroken for weeks."

She nodded seriously. "You are a sensitive type."

"Aren't you?" he asked.

She shook her head. "Uh-uh. Not like you."

"You have probed my weaknesses?"

She broke into a sunburst smile. "And found them very, very appealing. Oh Jon, can't you see, I wasn't looking for an affair, but I'm happy I met you. You're no Valentino...but then I think usually those men gamble and drink. They are vain, something you're not. Oh sure, Charles Egeny is the best poet this side of...this side of...Long Wharf, but that's different. That's a righteous kind of pride, has to do with paying witness to your talent, I do so respect and honor your talent and you are so sincere..." She finished by sweeping him into a kiss that brought them down together onto the moss.

He pulled up harshly. "Don't make me feel you think I'm so perfect and sincere."

Eyes half-closed, she sought him with weak fingertips. He took the fingertips of her left hand in the palm of his hand and squeezed.

"Ouch!" she exclaimed and looked at him terrified. "Let go!"

He released her fingers and threw himself on his back.

She hovered by him, her elegant features pale. "I was just...I wanted to possess you for a moment."

"Was that it?" He spoke sharply, then closed his eyes and placed his arms behind his head, hating himself for whatever she stirred in him.

Her fingertips played at a patch of moss on a rock, like picking a scab. "I think someday you are going to hate me."

"Sometimes I think you babble bullyshilly from that nutso colony in Fairfield."

She stared. So it was class warfare now.

He rose onto one elbow. "Look, I'm sorry. I don't care what those hyenas do or say. As a teenager I remember we used to pass through Westport…whenever they had a block dance for you spoiled brats…they used to throw us out on sight. West Haven kids. Blauugghh!"

"What's gotten into you?"

"Poetry! That's what! Can't you see? I'm not sure Charles Egeny is going to make it out of the slum. He'll write poetry, yes, and maybe publish a few things in tiny editions without pay, just to see his name in a byline, but ten years from now will he still be picking his nose while you and Mr. Kangaroo Bones are sipping cocktails in some high falootin congress of archeologists?"

She jumped to her feet. "Goddammit, that's about all I'm going to take! You're trying to typecast me because you're an insecure bastard! I haven't pulled any airs with you! You…you…lawn-mower!" She whirled and ran past the motionless green pond water toward the cleft between pines and cliffs where an overview of gray and white rooftops hid.

He rose to his feet, cursing, and stood looking into the glowing emerald pond. Balling his fists, he grimaced and uttered a bellowing scream that echoed among the rocks. Then he sat down, nervously pulling out tufts of grass from between his legs and throwing them over the water. The first mosquitoes, bumbling, small, and blind, hovered over the surface. The emerald mirror stench rose into his sinuses. He looked over and saw Merile sobbing, overlooking the houses.

"Can I say or do anything?"

She turned. "It doesn't matter."

He threw more moss onto the water. "It's no problem. It doesn't matter. How long will we know each other anyway?" He snapped his mouth shut, remembering her bracelet.

She walked to him. "Did I say something I shouldn't have?"

He threw up his arms. "God no. I'm sorry. It was my stupid thinking, that's all. My emotions. I'm fighting this battle, you see, about losing you. The more I want to hold you, the more I know I'll lose you."

She knelt beside him. "Maybe we should just call it quits. We can divvy up the picnic lunch down there and say it was a day."

He crushed his eyes shut. "No."

Her hand stole along his ear. In a very soft voice she whispered, "Will you stay a while?"

He reached up and pulled her down so she rolled over him and came to rest with reaching arms on his left. He pelted her with kisses and she sought his lips with her teeth. He reached down and his hand stole under her panties to grasp her round soft buttock. "I'm going to spread your legs and shove inside you."

"Yes." She whacked him on the back alternately with each of her palms.

He felt her kick her ankles asprawl, felt her muscles and flesh quiver as she did so.

As he took her, he knew she was taking him, and he delved between her long sprawling legs oblivious of all commitments to the contrary.

She bawled again, with her pink mouth wide open but no tears this time from her eyes squeezed shut. "I want you in me, I love you, forever, Jonathan Egeny Poetry Fuck, I don't want anyone to take you away from me, I love you so much."

I am going to lose myself in you, the orgasm of life and death, as if I throw myself into that pond and drown, and you will be my last thought in this universe, I want you so much.

They clawed at one another, relishing the moment and the glory, turning anger into sexual energy while the afternoon sun began to glare straight down and irradiate the pond so its fronds and slimy surface became dimly visible. That sun was the driver of all life, the engine of existence for carbon-based DNA complexity, replicative and iterative processes of complex organic reaction chains and other explosive realities, like the intersection of Jon and Merile.

This is life: a love affair; something beautiful growing in a place it isn't meant to, a doomed lovely flower we could cry over as it's meant to wilt and die just when it is so beautiful and filled with life.

Crickets shrilled in the prickly bushes. Flies and other insects began a milling flight pattern more complex than that of an international airport. Bubbles fermented to the surface of the pond, and spider-legged insects walked on the surface in search of prey. A bullfrog chirruped mournfully in some shady glen of leaves.

Jon and Merile sagged sweatily at the exhaustion of their sex. Their skin stuck together in the heat. They rolled apart to let air between their steamy bodies.

Some brief thrashing noise in the forest startled her. He had not heard it, but she sat up, pulling her dress down to her knees. "You'd better put on your clothes," she whispered.

He rolled lazily into a sitting position, listening into the forest, but could hear nothing. Clothing was scattered around them on the warm rocks.

She reached far to retrieve her panties, which she used to dry herself. He dried himself with his own and then dressed, feeling drained and finished and lethargic. The tension was not gone between them. Like the unmoving air, it hung between them. On a far ledge, he spotted a copperhead snake sleeping in noon sunlight.

I could start again, and take you, and again, and you would welcome me with open arms and legs. I would lose myself in you and never regret it for a moment. Except this is not ours to give or take. We are playthings as fate decrees.

He led her up the hill and down the other side, in the shadowy but hot woods, holding out a hand which she accepted wordlessly to help her down. As they approached the car, she stuffed her damp panties into his backpack. The secret of her nakedness under the skirt still excited him as it had during their ascent.

"Maybe they had the same idea," she said listlessly, pointing to a small white car pulled in among the woods some distance up the road. "Are you hungry?"

They shared sodas and baloney sandwiches, a lunch he had insisted on, kiddish and traditional. She grimaced at the taste of mustard and warm baloney.

The raspberry-chemical drink burned his throat.

She said, "I could have packed ham sandwiches and wine."

"I'm sorry. It was a dumb idea."

"It was the rule for picnics as you see them." She shrugged and grinned. "I went along with it, though."

"Live and learn," he admitted contritely while she made that vulnerable, sultry, wounded face. He saw that distant look, and imagined her gaze was directed far away at Mr. Cigar and what she must endure. "I'll make it better."

She looked up, suddenly sunshine, as if he had promised to be a better husband.

Summer heat softened slightly in its intensity as he pulled the car out onto the oozing tarry road surface. A breeze bringing with it smells of hot tar and lukewarm leaf juice rattled softly under the tattered cloth top of the faltering car. The car seemed to find its own way back toward New Haven. They rode in an engorged silence. "Shall we go to a movie?" he offered, but his voice sounded unconvincing even to him.

She shook her head and said "I'd rather not, I think. I'm sort of tired and in a mood to take a long soak in the tub."

About five minutes later they entered the outskirts of New Haven. She touched his arm. "Jon, I don't want you to be mad, but I don't want to see you for a while. I'm not saying never again, though maybe I should. I don't want our lives to get any more tangled."

He submitted with a mix of reluctance and relief. "We get too dramatic together."

She shook him by the shoulders. "It's all okay. We've known each other for such a short time, and it's been so intense—I've been wondering when we'd have some sort of blow-up."

He frowned in sunlight. "Charles Egeny hasn't written a really powerful poem in weeks."

"All this happiness makes you soft." She looked out over the passing green lawns and elm trees. "You can't let your own things go, you know." She grinned and added, "Can't let your friend the poet down."

He turned the corner slowly onto her street. "I really need some time to take care of things I've neglected."

"Like your buddies," she said sympathetically and sensibly. "Your poetry. Your dreams."

As he pulled up at the curb, she reached over the seat to gather her bag with picnic remains and various books and extra clothing.

He manfully removed the cooler and carried it to the house for her. They ascended the dark, cool stairway in silence. He waited for her familiar fumbling with keys.

Then the apartment door opened and he followed her into the dwelling. More than ever, he felt guilty and ungainly, an intruder, relishing the freshly painted and book-filled quiet and neatly ordered young/oldness of the apartment. Setting the cooler with its sloshing water and sliver-sized ice cubes in the sink, he walked into the living room with his hands in his pockets.

She emerged from the bedroom where she'd gone to put her unused sweater and book. She walked slowly, hands in the pockets of her skirt, kicking off her white deck shoes as she walked.

He was pointedly aware that she had nothing on underneath. "I'll go home and take a shower," he said.

"I hope Charles Egeny will write some poetry soon." Her smile was pointed and wistful. Her eyes were not without tenderness, yet an unconditional *something* hovered in her gaze, directing what must be done.

He felt relieved that he'd be leaving her. "I think it's long overdue."

"I'm expecting a phone call from Bill," she said. He called her every Saturday evening at five. As if she'd suddenly remembered, she sat dutifully on the couch beside the phone. She became insular and withdrawn.

Jon sat down on the couch about two feet away. "Look, I'm not going to kiss you goodbye, okay?"

She cast a minute glance in his direction. It was a dull, veiled, hurt look.

He said, "I'm realizing that I have no business kissing you goodbye. I mean we've shared our time. And all. I just. Oh, well, maybe you understand what I'm trying to say." She was someone else's wife into whose life he had briefly and ludicrously intruded.

Should he seal their dead-end relationship with a kiss or just turn his back? Somehow, it seemed, any gesture now would be to sanction a thing that should not have happened. A gesture would take away the thinly worn accidentalness with which they had both approached their liaison. It had been little more than a flirtation, a licentious thought, until that angry moment by the pond. Somehow things had gotten complicated at that very moment.

He started to rise, but with a swish of clothing she moved suddenly, putting her arms around his waist and resting her head in his lap...only briefly.

She sat up and took his hands between hers. "It's meant something." She whispered rapidly and her smile was only a half-smile, torn between emotions. "I wanted to push you out the door, but somehow I can't do it alone. When you leave I'll be glad you're out. I know what you're trying to say. I had a little forest pond to myself, before you plopped in like a big old rock and disturbed everything.

Now the water is full of ripples and I'm almost dreading this phone call today. I think it would be best if you don't come anymore. But I would like it if you would give me a kiss before you go."

He kissed her cheek, but it wasn't enough. Smelling her hair, seeing her eyes flutter shut and her lips open, breath bated, he hovered on the brink of sinking down on the couch with her. In that moment he respected her weakness and rose, pulling her to her feet. She moved readily as he directed, eyes still closed, hair tangled and fuzzy, lips slightly parted in an expression of exquisite want and hurt.

He took her hand as if she were a doll and led her to the door. She padded along, unknowing and confused. Her bare feet padded quietly on the cool, glossy wood floor.

At the door, she clung to him. He embraced her tightly, kissing her, and he ran his hand along her waist, down to her buttocks, feeling the material of her dress slide loosely over bare, electric skin.

She stiffened and pulled away.

He unlocked the door and started into the hallway.

Her hands reached for his arm, caught it briefly, then released it.

He plunged into the dark stairwell on wing-borne feet, giving a last spastic wave to her shocked and indistinct face hovering around a closing door, and then he was out on the porch, feet pounding on the hot wood, down on the concrete, in the car, struggling with a whining starter, and off in a screech of tires which he knew he shouldn't as he pulled away down the sleeping street, turning the corner sharply to get away from its crinkling elm leaves and sad, knowing, owl-windowed houses.

Chapter 8

The night of his departure from the owl-eyed street, he would have a battle all alone with moths high in his garret room. But first—it was still daylight before then, and he was filled with the purpose of picking up dropped threads.

For the first time in several weeks, he drove out to his parents' house in West Haven, arriving just as streetlights came on in the inky-blue evening. Crickets chirped in the remainder of raccoon- and turtle-filled tidal swamps as he knocked. The door was as always radiant with a friendly amber light. Good old milk box, good old dog house, good old trees, good old door handle, good old moths ticking blindly against the brick wall and the milky lamp cover.

Good old air conditioning. They three alone ate in the den while the TV flickered and the potatoes looked blue. His father, wearing Bermuda shorts and a crinkled white shirt whose buttons were laden with the weight of his belly hairs, sat enthroned in the easy chair with a seven-and-seven at hand. His mother, a small, wiry woman with her jet-black hair in curlers, sat beside Jon on the couch as they ate calmly.

"How about school in the fall?" his father asked after dinner, kneading his fingers and peering at Jon with discomfitingly direct, gleaming eyes while Merv Griffin sat back laughing on the black-and-white TV.

Jon shrugged. "I've thought about it. I'm making decent money and I may put it off for a year. Save some money, you know, get a bigger apartment." It was a lie, sadly; he knew Charles Egeny would demand periods of dissolute artistry in which no money could be saved.

His mother said, "Are you going to continue in your major?" It was a reproving question requiring a negative answer.

He shook his head. "There is a good MBA program at Wesleyan."

"What about UConn?" his father asked.

"I'm looking for something different," he said. "I need a total change."

"Do you think you can handle business and accounting?" his mother asked.

"I'll have to take the Graduate Record Exams first, of course." Jon Harney, if not Charles Egeny, was practical minded. He had no idea if he could do well on the GRE.

"That sounds a little more like it," said his father, a smart fellow, lately working as a mill foreman supervising the extrusion of stinking rubber at a nearby tire factory. His father, a product of the Depression, hadn't had the chance to go to college. His good mind and sound body had been carefully harnessed over the years to the task of raising a family and providing a comfortable, if small, home in a middle-class suburb which forty years earlier had been swamp land and farm country.

"We just wish you the best," his mother said.

They were easy-going, understanding parents. They understood struggle, though they little realized it could exist in the form of poetry. He could attach no formula of rebellion to his departure from their enclosed world. They had married when his father was nineteen, his mother sixteen. Perhaps the one benefit of this premature liaison was that today they were still young enough to enjoy the relative calm as their children moved beyond adolescence.

It was too quiet around the house, and he rose, saying he was going out. "Try to stop by or call a little more often," his father told him as they saw him to the door.

"And remember there's always a room here for you if you need a place to sleep," his mother added anxiously.

"Mom!" he admonished. After kissing her, he re-entered the night and dove back into his own life.

He drove reasonably and calmly through the narrow avenues of beaches and wind-swept trees he'd known all his life. Long Island Sound glittered under a field of stars. On a distant groin, a beacon swirled across galaxies—as if sailors from distant Aldebaran or Fomalhaut were in danger of running aground off—like—Charles Island or Montauk.

The ultimate dropped thread was his desk far away in New Haven, he knew. He resisted the thrill of warm typewriter ink and fresh paper cooked to a buttery aroma by a hot summer night. First, he turned a familiar corner near the beach and parked before a hedge-hidden house. Leaving his car at the curb, he rang the doorbell and stood waiting on a porch of laid brick, with amber light and moths, not unlike that of his parents.

The aluminum screen door revealed the approach of a tall, slender figure trailing gossamer house colors. Long black hair dangled glossy around a pale face with delicate pink lips and dark eyes. "Hi, how are you?" came the muted squeal of sincere pleasure from Dawn Ferraro.

He gave her a brotherly wink, to which she responded with familiarity, even a cool fondness. She was his best friend's sister, which made even the thought of her as a woman seem offensive and incestuous. Not surprisingly, she seemed as stimulated by him as by an old car on blocks. "Is Andy home?"

She rubbed her hands in concern. "No…" She shouted over her shoulder, "Mom, where's Andy?" A distant voice answered. Jon could have reached through the screen and hugged her, loving these people and their familiar voices.

Welcome back to a normal existence.

"He's out on a date," Dawn said regretfully, wringing her hands on a dish towel. "Want to come in?"

He felt slightly relieved. He'd done his duty and made this initial gesture of re-establishment of contact with his old high school friend. He shook his head. "I know he's probably mad I haven't called. I'll head on back to my apartment. Can you tell him I called? Ask him to call me? If he calls tomorrow I'll stop by tomorrow night!"

He drove away from the beach, headed through the poorer outskirts of the city. He had nothing to lose here and drove through rapidly, thinking of the several phone numbers secreted in his wallet from meetings in meat racks and not-so-meat racks (bars frequented by college students rather than divorcées) in recent months. Satisfied with the evening's picking up of threads, he resolved now to explore the world of Charles Egeny, left delinquent for weeks.

The city was enchanted with lights, betraying the bitter truth of its pocket ghettoes. It was an old city, and in other pockets survived remnants of its past as a slumbering colonial dame. Coursing amid squinting streetlights rubbed by leafy elm branches, he was touched for a moment by the irony of the fact that Merile's apartment was a scant six blocks from his own.

His street, as leafy and owl-eyed as any, nestled amid parks and schools on the border into Hamden, a five-minute walk from Edgerton Park, in the shadow of East Rock whose illumined red flanks shot teasingly into the clear sky, surmounted by a celebrative column visible for miles.

Putting up the top and sealing the windows of his car, he mounted the long, creaking steps to the fourth floor of the rambling house in which he shared an apartment with two Yale students.

He emerged into darkness. He flickered the light switch. Morose illumination spattered a central living room, which was no more a living room than their apartment was a home. He barely knew the names of his two fellow tenants. As was often the case, both roommates were out. In the refrigerator in their shared kitchen he found several bottles of inexpensive California red wine, left from a party he'd helped co-sponsor, but never showed up at.

He took a steamy shower in the shared bath, reminded of separate, territorial masculinities as he smelled three distinct shaving creams stacked on individual shelves.

Toweling himself dry, he regretted that the place did not have an air conditioner. The summer night was not yet airless, oppressively sticky, and sweaty. Nevertheless, he turned on the oscillating fan as he entered his small room with the steep garret roof. His room: A bed, under the louvered ceiling; a bureau filled with rumpled underwear and unironed shirts; a steamer trunk filled with manuscripts and untouched books; a chair, a desk, and a typewriter. One poster adorned a limply wallpapered wall: the Manhattan skyline, with a soaring Concorde superimposed over a verdigrised Statue of Liberty. Charles Egeny would one day be famous there.

A wall of loneliness engulfed him as he sat at the typewriter. Three moths coursed about the open lamp nearby. A fourth moth buzzed in the glowing trough of light, fanning itself into extinction while its fellows danced about. He had brought a bottle of cold Gallo from the kitchen, its glass in icy tears, and poured a tangy few ounces. With eager fingers, he pulled paper onto platen.

He tried hard, but only crap came out—no sexy rhythm, no jazz, no undercurrents, nor sensuous *entendres*. The typewriter clattered dustily in the night. Somewhere a window clapped shut. He stopped and looked through the torn screen window, through a great conifer, at the brilliant diadem of yellow lights of a residential building across the street. In one apartment, a party with raucous laughter was in progress. Somewhere else, a wistful hand bricked out sequential piano thoughts which rose disconnected through pine sap. A mosquito hawk's shadow bumbled in fast zigzag motions on the tilted ceiling. The wine was tart and cold: stored Pacific coastal sunshine.

Clattering, the typewriter echoed over the street and he stopped and took another sip of wine.

Nothing. What's missing is my baby's loving eyes.

Charles Egeny was not here tonight. Where was he? With Merile while he, fool, labored here? No such luck even. He hosed down wine as if putting out a fire. The typewriter, dull and black, soaked in his thoughts like a Black Body in space. He exerted sweat beads of force to drive home phrases ringing with irony and contrapuntal inventiveness. *From the eye to the ear...* Charles Olson had written, tracing the electric flow of poetic music.

This hot typewriter, resentfully steeping these past weeks in sunshine and driven motes, absorbed all that nurture and belched forth not a spare syllable of meaningful reverie. The seat of his pants grew glued to the unkind, borrowed seat of the chair.

In a window obscured by plastic blinds, a feminine form undressed. Not knowing she was on stage, she innocently cast filmy white garments onto a cold bed. He sat frozen at his typewriter, watching and afraid to tap out another key sound, as pink nipples dangled into/

—and then, as Jon stared hypnotically, her light went out. Whoever she might be, she went to bed alone, or so he fretted. She was unaware that here a man sat listlessly sucking in puckersome quantities of bloody grape ferment, wishing their destinies could be briefly twinned.

That special gift comes only once in an age.

The glass met the desk top hard, but did not break. He weaved, sitting. Like a fish in an ocean of night, he gulped cobwebs. Those moths had multiplied. He gestured feebly to keep them off the blank page, but one great juicy green buck with majestically flapping, dirty-bedsheet wings hovered obsessively, almost angrily. With a twirl of the platen, this noble pilot turned a color like the speckling of sparse black hatchings on the page, where he'd tried to summon Charles Egeny, conqueror of the skyline and the torch-waving statue. It got late and the party ended; not a single nipple beckoned pinkly nor ironically behind any more slatted windows. He heaved himself out of the glued chair with a rip of sat-on skin and staggered to the bathroom. Flailing drunkenly, he aimed a heavy piss at the porcelain crapper. Alone in the oppressive garret heat, he wended his way into the room again. There, gulping and gasping amid a sea of flailing dirty-white moth wings, he sank sideways into a stupor.

* * * *

The indignant mosquito-like keening of his dirty-white alarm clock, coupled with a damp, cold, greasy wind on his bare back, summoned him into gray dawn. Heavy-headed, he swung into a sitting position and enumerated the ways in which a Sonoma red wine could taste muffy, fluffy, nauseous, and thirst-burning the morning after.

Jon Harney stumbled on aching feet over the dusty wooden floor into the kitchen where thankfully a pitcher of ice water was in the refrigerator. He quaffed deeply, draining perhaps a quart from its echoic hull. He'd read that most of one's taste comes from smell buds. There it was: he winced in distaste at a rankling descent into ripeness and over-ripeness of variously refrigerated baloney and onions and browned lettuce.

Ahh… thus a bachelor pad, or what say ye?

He was on time for work. Wiping condensation from the car windows and stepping into its moldering artificial interior, he sought the ordered rhythms of work.

Let there be lawn mowing and hedge trimming.

The growing day's warmth would dispel the soggy corona of a summer stored in bloody wine—all too briefly a summer's resigned hope.

He was summoned into the tiled and damp interior of the foreman's supply room where Armand Artiglio rested a grim mien and a pudgy thigh upon a worn dark wood desk. "I hate to tell you the bad news, son, but there's no putting it off. There has been a cutback in funds and naturally since you are the lowest on the union list you are affected directly." Armand, wearing checkered pants and a dark blue windbreaker, nervously shuffled papers—which needed no shuffling—on his desk .

"Wait a minute," said Jon Harney, struggling not to drop his cup of acrid and rubbery-smelling machine coffee.

"I'm sorry," Armand said afraid to meet his eyes. The hard, distanced look, the stanced attitude, in Artiglio's eyes threatened the rest of what had to be said.

"You can pick up your pink slip at the union office," Armand said, shuffling his papers aimlessly. "Even though you ain't one of the union."

"I understand," Jon Harney said, leaving his coffee steaming on the hard chipped desk as he rose and started wonderingly out of the tiled office.

As he left, he saw in the fuzzy environs of Armand Artiglio's office a darkly coiffeured man of indeterminate age, wearing a frown and a dashing gray suit.

This had been set up cutely. His next step should have been the union. Since he had not worked here long enough to qualify for membership, that would gain nothing. The union steward, a balding little man with conspiratorial eyes and ever so boyish cynicism, passed him in the parking lot; probably no accident; a gesture of sympathy, "Sorry…"

* * * *

Jon Harney paused under a cloudy skyline and surveyed his ruined thoughts.

As he stood on the street, numbly, almost guilty because right about now he should have been sitting on the assignment truck with the rakes and lawnmowers, he saw that silent man leaving the office: tiptoeing on hushed & puppied soles, his suede-patch elbows raised at an indignant angle, shoulders hunched so his school tie dangled, Ivy

League mane scraping his collar, and dark eyes peering poisonously; so Jon Harney perceived him. After that fraction of a glance, the man entered a little yellow Le Car (license plate KD5978) and tooled away into the dense traffic. Jon started speculatively after the little yellow car, memorizing its license plate.

Survival before information: Jon had a quick cup of coffee and planned a strategy to avoid both starvation and depression. A quick check of the newspaper revealed that "20 men were needed right away" and all that sort of thing, but unless you had experience in a trade or profession it was clearly an uphill fight to land a beginning job. He left the paper in a trash can and went to the employment office. Between there and the unemployment office, he wasted precious time well into the afternoon.

Well, there's always the taxi company if all else fails.

It was nearly five in the afternoon when he pulled to a stop outside his apartment on Edgerton Street. He had no appetite, but forced himself to eat a cheap chef salad in a small air-conditioned diner downtown. The city—emptying of its daytime multitude of suburban working people—took on a sleepy, bated empty atmosphere in-between time. It was Happy Hour in the bars.

Here's proof: there is really an Unhappy Hour.

At night, a totally different sort of traffic coursed through its old veins, but it wasn't dark yet. He escaped the stifling heat and basking streets, relieved that the day's struggle was over, almost happy to say to himself he'd done enough and enter the leafy, sunlit half-world of suppertime in the city's residential areas.

In the quiet, breezy stairwell of the building in which he lived, Jon opened the fourth-floor mail box and sifted through envelopes large and small. The mail of his fellow renters aroused in him a mix of jealousy, boredom, and joy.

He was jealous because a lot of their mail, related to their job-seeking, came from important-sounding firms eager to draft Yalies.

He was bored by the company names—dry-sounding law firms, conglomerated canners, incorporated shoe design, creative wretches, executive searchers, and the like.

He was downright joyous at times that he wasn't interested in hooking up with Undulant Design, Marketing Associates, cardboard box manufacturers in Montana, a chemical company in Jersey, or anything else redolent of Gray Flannel Suits.

In the mailbox were several items for him. One was a postcard from Aunt Mavis, aged sixty-seven, in Bermuda; she sent love and kisses, and he nodded to her in spirit.

He found two bills to pay, and an offer to join a book club. The Randolph R. Bumsted Poetry Society's current offering was *Delphic Zones* by one Ziskin DelShoot. After scoffing, he decided such an esoteric name would properly baffle his roommates, even make them jealous and curious. He stuffed the item back into the common mail box out of spite.

Ah! Here was a big manila envelope addressed to him by his misspelled name John, from The Booker, Publishers Inc. They were, at the moment, a key poetry publisher in the U.S.. He tore the envelope open with trembling fingers. It had been six months since he'd submitted 25 poems. He sat down on the stair step and read:

Dear JH: You write well and show much promise. However, you should know that publishing is a flihty business. Your poetry is genuine and full of a haunting classical quality and I imagine maybe we could have published. Our editors for the most part wanted to say yes but then came the marketing folks and they tell me we couldn't possibly go ahead with an unknown. So you'll have to keep trying with the magazines until your name becomes famous. If you're still interested by then. My advice is keep trying. Don't quit your day job.

Best wishes, KNG

Charles Egeny read and re-read the letter with outrage and disbelief.

What in hell is a flihty business?

He tried to read between the lines but there was nothing there which was clear.

Did they say these things in every rejection slip?

Should he try them again, or should he simply keep trying every publisher in general and not them in particular?

Is publishing a flighty or a flitty or a filthy business?

The typos annoyed him. Who was KNG? Some sweaty elf in a business suit who was afraid to commit himself even when he thought the writer was 'genuine' and 'haunting' and 'classical.' Finally the Catch-22, namely, they wouldn't publish you if you didn't have a name and you couldn't get a name unless you were published.

"You idiots," he said to himself, walking heavily up the stairs.

Stallion, his black typewriter, like everything else in his room, sat where Charles Egeny had left him.

Still wearing his shoes, he threw himself across the bed, rumpled bed sheets only half covering the striped mattress. Somewhere a stereo was throbbing.

He drifted heavily into sleep.

Chapter 9

A telephone waited in fingerprinted, dusty repose under a rubber palm tree in the Dohertys' apartment. Stifling summer air penetrating to its quiet perch took on a hopeful, seeking, delicately probing quality. Having neither lungs nor taste buds nor soul, however, the telephone receiver, rarely ever rung, responded to this organic stimulus by stolidly sitting between the involuted globules of its handset.

When the air had achieved a late-afternoon fullness, the apartment door opened, then closed. A pocketbook sailed rapidly and briefly to a landing in the cotton and dust of an easy chair. Hands struggled with high-heeled shoes that dropped heavily to the wood floor. Bare feet padded on the glossy wood floor (one might have choreographed a dance of liberation from sweltering office routine) and fingers rustled in cotton clothing which swished in being removed over long limbs. Cotton clouds sighed to the floor as bare feet padded onto the linoleum kitchen floor and then the tile bathroom floor and then there was the rattle of water on enamel, made hollow by the acoustics of a bathtub and the snare drum of a shower curtain.

The telephone reposed under the rubber palm, subject to the waxy brushings of the palm's large, gnawed-looking leaves. An electrical impulse quickened as the telephone—receiving hints of a sweaty, nervous, importuning emotion far away—prepared to ring.

Shower water turned off. Dozens of small needle jets stopped striking printed flowers on a snare drum plastic curtain. Nothing followed. Two minutes later, the curtain rattled aside on brass rings. A tile floor whispered with wet footprints and water spatters.

In the living room, the phone shrilled over hardwood, ending a long, cruel stillness.

Bare feet padded quickly on the floor, leaving damp prints on the linoleum and then on the wood. A terrycloth towel made a muffled snapping sound, drawn over a long, slender back. A hand with long fingers still moist under the fingertips picked up the receiver.

A male voice crackled, "Mrs. Doherty?"

Merile said, "Yes?"

"Charley Anderson from the Archie Department. You know, the Susskinds' party? My wife wore the orchid?"

"Yes?" Slightly harried, she sat on the armrest of the easy chair, her dangling breasts beaded with stray droplets, as she strove to wrap the towel up around her sopping hair.

"I was just headed home from the office and I thought I might stop by and drop off some mail for your husband."

She laughed to herself in relief, having feared an invitation to another party. At these parties were always a collection of wives, ranging from the orchid-wearing to the mousy or brassy-voiced, engaged in irrelevant but feelingful subterranean clashes. She'd inevitably just as well see smiling dons in their hushed puppies and carefully unkempt tweeds—worn these days with suede elbow patches—once a plaintive sign of undergraduate poverty, nowadays an understated symbol of overstated status. She recalled seeing maids and servants tendering cocktails; colleagues with tactical smiles and carefully hoarded cleverness; and, amid all that, one or two queer-eyed, suntanned, dirty-fingernailed field workers like Bill, briefly back from the actual work.

She said, "Sure, Mr.—ah—Anderson, when?"

"How about a—*haha*, right now?"

She frowned. It sounded as though he'd licked his lips.

"Will you be there this evening?" he asked.

She frowned. *Do I detect...?* "Why yes, if you think it's important," she said.

He (she could feel his moist smile) said, "I'll just stop by in about fifteen minutes."

What's just stopping by versus stopping by?

She hurried to finish drying herself. Left her hair in that turban for drying later, under the fan, combing it, while moths ticked against the screen window. Slipped on sheer panties and a bra (which she did not care to wear around the house). And left her housecoat by the door like a suit of armor (not of *amour*).

Chapter 10

H ey!" Feeling himself being shaken, Jon Harney raised his head groggily and peered. His mangled bed sheets and striped mattress were wet with sweat and unpleasant dreams.

Andy Ferraro heaved his long, thin, muscular frame onto the bed. "Wake up, man. Get with it."

Jon wiped sleep from his eyes. He sat up, suddenly refreshed and happy. "Hey. I'm glad you stopped by."

Andy Ferraro, twenty-four, was a philosophy graduate and currently bartender by profession, and coincidentally a drily vulgar comedian. "*Putan*'. Get out of that crappy bed, you loser. I thought it was going to be another hundred years before I ever heard from you again, you dipshit."

Jon stood and stretched. It was evening. The clock read seven p.m. "I slept for a few hours. I got fired today. Had a rough day."

Andy regarded him with quizzical blue eyes in a round face under reddish-blond hair. "Wha' hoppen?"

Jon shrugged. "Just laid off, I guess." Groggily he searched for towel and soap. "Hope you don't mind."

"Got anything to read while I wait?"

Jon pointed to a stack of racy magazines.

"What are you giving me these for?"

"Your level of mentality."

"Thanks. You know why we have two eyes and women have two tits." He had a very dry, understated sense of humor, served on a heaping plate of Italian sounding vulgarities and ironies. His degree was in philosophy; his practical application in life (thus far) at the philosophical fountain of spiritude (bartending).

"Evolution. So we can see each other."

"Yes. Survival. Women have two eyes and we have a cock. Makes absolutely no sense."

"That's called a triangle."

"Very complex geometry." Andy's eyes gleamed with a mix of humor and concupiscence as he sifted through the magazines looking for a cover that interested him. "You know that I only read these for the articles."

"I have never actually looked in one," Jon lied as he stepped into the bathroom and wrapped himself in the steam and hot water of a rehabilitative shower.

The door opened and shut as Andy came to sit atop the crapper cover with a copy of *Playboy*. "Do women like this really exist?"

Jon Harney soaped himself. "Nah. Not in real life."

I've just been in love and lust with one.

"Hey, are you screwing some married bitch?"

Jon sputtered through soap bubbles, "Where'ju hear that?"

O my god, what now. Who else knows? Mr. LeCar? Some oily faculty fuck trying for a shot at Merile for himself, thinking she must be cheap?

"Simple deduction," Andy said. "I didn't hear from you for the longest time, ergo you were getting laid regularly. You weren't bragging, ergo it's illegal."

Jon rinsed himself. "She'd take your breath away."

"You were seen downtown," Andy said.

"By who?"

"By whom?" Andy corrected. "My sister. She says she saw you pawing each other; some chick out of a fashion magazine."

"It's all over now," Jon said, rinsing. "God am I glad it's over ."

"Who is she?" Andy asked.

Jon turned off the water and reached blindly for a towel. "Some Yale professor's wife." He found a towel.

"You have balls like a brass monkey statue."

Jon pulled aside the curtain. "Small town, isn't it?"

Can't keep any secrets here.

Andy shrugged. His shrug implied the distance between townie types and university types, between whom over the centuries there had been little empathy.

Jon dried himself and they migrated to the tangled bedroom. He told Andy, "Don't ever get involved with a married woman. It's hell on the emotions."

Andy looked up from the magazine. "Don't I know it?" Andy had the past winter involved himself with a waitress from the Beverly Inn at which he'd been tending bar. The upshot had been that the waitress, who was resigned to being beaten regularly by her husband, gave Andy a case of clap presumably obtained from her husband, and that Andy had lost his job after being seen with the guy's wife by another member of the bricklayer's union or something. "This is your first adventure, isn't it?" Andy asked.

"The first and last," Jon declared, dressing.

"Smart move," said Andy with utter conviction.

"It doesn't lead to anything," Jon said as they drove in Andy's modified Camaro into the center of New Haven, where at the moment the last stanzas of a carillon concert from the Hearkness Memorial Tower clattered in ever so wistful melody. Big bells elsewhere might proclaim boldly, but precious little Meriles like these lisped in hesitant, cute phrasings.

I ache for her.

At Jon's request, they passed through a small side street in which Jon knew the department of Archeology was housed. Sure enough, there was a small LeCar, KD5978, parked beside the meter.

"Drive on," Jon said.

Andy said, "What do you say we take a drive down along Milford Beach?"

"Anything," Jon said.

Andy brought the Camaro into high gear. "I hear the chicks down there are ripe and ready."

"Sounds like the pinkest and ripest thing to do," said Jon, stiffly sitting upright in his bucket seat as if he'd just been in an bicycle accident with a beer truck.

Andy grinned as they headed for the distant, dusky suburb of Milford where the surf was known to seethe around slender bathing bodies, feminine in nature.

As highway air rattled through the cloth-top Camaro, Jon tried to put aside feelings of guilt and apprehensiveness. What would this Mr. LeCar do to Merile's husband's career? What would happen when Merile's husband found out?

I want to hold you, rock you, shelter you in my arms.

Chapter 11

The doorbell rang, and Merile rose quickly from a flickering TV screen to don her house robe.

When Merile opened the door—knotting the belt of her house coat, conscious of the ungainly turban about her head—she found a short, stocky man with a smile standing before her. He had dark hair, bald on top, and an ingratiating smile; he wore a shirt and tie and hash-guppy shoes; his tweedy jacket bore the unmistakable sign of current collegiate fashion in that its sleeves had leather elbow patches. He held a sheaf of papers and bowed slightly. "Charley Anderson."

"Won't you come in?" she said reluctantly.

He swam into the apartment, wearing a mixed halo of academic respectability and lip-licking intent which no woman could mistake. But he was an older man, and subtle if not sneaky. "What a hot day! I am parched."

"I have some cold water," she said and went to the kitchen.

"That would be fine," he allowed.

She served him bottled water in a dripping, raspberry-colored glass. They sat in the living room, he on the couch and she strategically on a backless stool. She thought of England's island position in European politics. Evidently he was unconsciously picturing himself as Norman France, ready to invade. He held his glass in both hands like a potion tainted, if one cared to explore Shakespeare. "And how are you, Mrs. Doherty?" he said.

"Oh I'm fine," she responded vaguely, toweling her hair and careful not to expose more than her ankles.

He carefully suppressed his nervous anxiety. "I came here on a rather sensitive mission," he said.

"I am a sensitive woman," she admonished.

"How true," he said. "What I meant to get at. Well, Mrs. Doherty, what I meant to get at. Well, it's certainly a warm evening isn't it. Mrs. Doherty, what I meant to get at."

She fanned herself.

He reiterated, holding his glass in both hands, "What I was going to say. Mrs. Doherty, we of the university are a small community. That is, we are like a family." He paused to let this sentiment of closeness sink in. "We are devoted to the cause of archeology." He pronounced archeology like archaeo-ohology pronounced with needless extra syllables for pretentious effect. He said, "Our wives are part of this closely knit community. Now as you know, often husbands are called to esoteric corners of the earth by their careers. That is to say, wives are separated from their husbands for long periods of time. And of course this is a situation not very dissimilar to that of soldiers. That is, I mean to say, husbands and wives are separated for long periods of time. And of course at all the faculty gatherings, when the husband is gone, it is the wife who is expected to fill in for him. Now this implies more than just what happens at parties. In any case, it is important to realize the effect a wife's actions can have upon her husband's career. Especially, that is, I mean to say, when the husband is far away on some vital field mission. Do you know what I mean?"

She answered his expectant pause with a casual comment, "You are not saying as much as you mean, and I suspect you mean more than you say."

You randy old pervert.

He put his glass aside and moved closer on the couch so that he was barely two feet from her. "Mrs. Doherty, may I call you Merile?"

He pronounced it like "I feel" and she wanted to go take a shower to get his taint off of her.

She shrugged, meaning more than she said.

No, you asshole.

He continued, "I am a very liberal-minded sort of fellow. In fact, I am an admirer of the free-minded spirits who have been known to grace the annals of our university. In short, if there has ever been a person who, as Assistant Chairman of the Department of Archaeohology, was willing to further the aims of the science, it is I. However, there are certain social restraints which are always important to the advancement of a talented individual within our field. I refer to well—how should I put it—the strenuous efforts of your husband in the field while of course all of us wait with bated breath to learn of his results. Merile, a small indiscretion on the part of the wife of such an individual could have a very negative effect on the results of such an individual's rise within the department. That is I mean to say, oh hell isn't it obvious Merile, your associations of late have not contributed favorably to your husband's career?"

She stretched languidly. "Oh?"

He smiled wretchedly. "Merile, my sweet dear little Merile, there is funding involved. As assistant department head, I can only be too painfully aware of circumstances which could lead to the cessation of funding and ultimately the suspension of a project due to the indiscretions of his loved ones."

She curled her wrists dangerously in the cotton of her turban. "So?"

He nudged her knee. "You are a very attractive woman."

She shrugged. "What's that mean?" she seemed to survey flocks of shit birds passing over the ceiling on a migration south—literally and figuratively.

He nudged anxiously, "You are a needful woman like any, aren't you?"

"You'll have to speak English if you know how."

He gestured secretively, "Your husband is going to be a famous man in our field someday. You wouldn't want his name besmirched by any allegations, would you?"

"What sorts of allegations?" she asked.

Are you accusing me of murder, because I'm about to beat you to death with an aluminum mixing bowl?

He inched closer and closer, physically and verbally. She could begin to smell his breath—an unbearable essence of toe jam. "Darling, you are a woman alone. I know you have been seeing a certain individual who mows lawns around the university."

"Serious allegation," she said.

You sick fuck.

He said, "Said individual has been terminated."

"I'm glad," she said.

Poor baby. My fault.

He shook his head, denying any gesture of denial. "I don't think you appreciate the seriousness of the situation."

She stared at him directly. "What exactly do you want?"

He broke down and the game was over. "You."

"Me."

If I could shut my sagging mouth, I could still not talk.

"Yes. I'd give anything." His eyes implored.

Will I be able to breathe again after he leaves?

She surveyed him. "Have you had your temperature taken lately?"

Will there still be oxygen?

He buried his face in his hands. "*Mereel.* The first time I saw you…"

She rose. "Get out of here."

He threw himself around her knees. "Please."

"Get out of here!" she bellowed. "One more word, and I will call the police."

"What will your husband say?" It was his final, feeble threat before he walked dazedly out the door. She listened to him on the stairs, fighting tears of rage, humiliation, and terror. She watched him out the window as he went to his car down on the street.

She tore open a window and hollered out the worst curse she could think of, "Go screw your wife if she'll have you!"

Chapter 12

Feeling bad about Mr. Le Car, Jon sat beside Andy in the Seven Winds Bar in Milford as they sipped beer. They had sounded the side streets of Milford through the early evening hours, until word had filtered somehow among the gray wood houses that there would be girls at the Seven Winds Bar.

Two young girls attached themselves. Andy went off to dance with Jane, the taller of the two. The bar thundered with loud rock music and the slap of ice being thrown into glasses by busy bartenders. It wasn't the sort of place where you ordered something fancy like a Rusty Nail or a Dubonnet on the rocks.

Jane's friend Alice was a slender young chick in blue corduroys pants and a double-knit sleeveless pink jersey that left her brown arms and shoulders exposed and barely veiled her heroically forward-pointing breasts. She was *Liberty Leading the Masses* in the famous painting of revolutionary France by Eugène Delacroix.

Alice and Jane were from Fairfield County. "What are you doing in this neck of the woods?" Jon asked.

Alice, with long auburn hair carefully washed and falling in a frilly tease over her brown shoulders, was all smiles and white teeth. "We just happened drive this way." Her attitude was guarded; her smile hovering very white against dark velvet skin in a black light glowing around the bar. Jon saw that Andy, on the dance floor, was having a struggle getting his arms fully around bodacious Jane. He wondered if they could each be much over seventeen.

"Do you often drive east this way?" Jon asked, conscious of the hundred jealous looks fastened upon Alice, who preened with adolescent queenliness.

"I just happened to get the Mercedes from my dad to go shopping," Alice said, smiling through braces.

"You don't get the Mercedes very often?" Jon asked indirectly, unprepared to indulge in a long and vague exchange of credentials.

A tall, muscular fellow hefting a beer bottle and wearing a stylish BVD shirt elbowed in close, casting lingering looks over the pale skin of young Alice.

Jon sipped intently at the beer on the bar before him, ignoring the wiry arms that rippled discreet warnings in his direction.

Alice turned glowing eyes upward and without apology departed in the sinuous embrace of one Marc, or was it Mark or even Marx? Seeing under ever-attentive brows the departure of Alice, Jane impulsively untangled herself from Andy's embrace and swooned in the direction taken by Marx and Alice.

"Bitches!" Andy remarked, finding his abandoned beer bottle and embracing it with clenched fingers.

Jon was thinking about Charles Egeny. "Say," he said, "I think I'll hand-carry my manuscript to New York."

"What are you talking about?" grumbled Andy.

"Nothing," Jon said. "Just talking to myself."

The music inside the Seven Winds grew louder. The air-conditioned atmosphere, filled with sweat and beer, grew more intense at the dance performed by Marx and Alice in a corner. Her milk-coffee skin and glowing face.

Someday, somewhere, someone, those breasts...

"Let's split, Andy."

Chapter 13

enuine and classical and sincere. He reread those words on the bus to New York City. They contrasted grayly with the sky-scraping apartments passed by the bus. He had this letter and the manuscript, and the letter was a note of rejection from a prominent publisher. It read something like, "Your voice has a power unrivaled in recent poetry. We like the elegant flow of your haunting and classical lines pertaining to the boredom of a faun in a garden filled with flowers and fountains. Unfortunately, we cannot accept your work because you are not a known poet."

Was it not time Jon Harney pulled a coup? He had this letter from a prominent publisher and wasn't it time he pressed the point, pushed the issue, tried to make his mark?

In the NY Port Authority he felt small and burdened; men in gray suits hurried about. Wasn't it time? He let lukewarm water run over his hands in a restroom of the Port Authority. Then he set out to find Everhard Eburgenhas, the publisher, and with some difficulty he located their offices in a building dedicated to the promulgation of marketing arts on the Avenue of the Americas. He found his way up an elevator, and there on the thirtieth floor were the front offices of Everhard Eburgenhas, biography unknown, who had pretensions of being a publisher of poetry.

Charles Egeny made his entrance there full of marveling and drenched with sweat from lowly streets.

The hall smelled of shoe polish, artificial carpeting, and books. Unlikely looking fellow poesans nodded politely to him as he stood outside the elevator wiping sweat from under his collar and soaking in the cooled air: An old lady in jogging shorts; a tall, gangling, balding man in a gray suit; a frail-looking white-haired priest who looked about eighty years old...

This then was the literary fountain in paradise of Everhard Eburgenhas, publisher and adept.

Jon approached the front desk, where a chubbyish-pretty young secretary typed.

"Hello," he said.

"Hi," she said readily, turning clean white sclera and teeth up at him above a purple dress matching her violet irises.

"I've come from New Haven and I was hoping to be able to speak with somebody."

"Well, who did you want to speak with?" she gushed.

He laid the manila envelope with Charles Egeny's collected poems on the desk. "I brought some poems...I really would appreciate..." He'd come to the brusque city prepared to climb in the editor's window if necessary. The commonly human nine-to-five air at Eburgenhas surprised him. These people were as human as he was. Where was the band with the 101 Trombones and all the sacred music?

She folded her arms together, regarding him with tolerant eyes. "Who in particular did you want to talk to?"

With whom did you want to speak? Andy, philosopher and transubstantiator of wine into the divine, would be all over this with ironic, mocking rhetoric.

He smiled uncertainly. Personally, he found her and how she talked cute—live jive, real people, real time. He wasn't prepared for her question. "Well, I...anyone, I guess, who reads poetry. I've published a few of my poems in various magazines, and I have the clippings with me."

She tisked. "Clippings! You shouldn't have cut your poems out!"

"Less paper to lug around," he protested. "It's a long trip, and hot out today."

"Poor guy. The water fountain is over there." She pointed, and Jon desperately dove to irrigate and cool the desert that his mouth had become. Were those cannon shots or heartbeats shaking the dunes?

She pressed a button at her side. "Mr. Chalmers, there is a young man with a manuscript—do you have a minute to speak with him?"

An answering noise crackled, sounding indistinct to Jon's anxious ears. The woman nodded encouragingly and pointed down the hallway.

John went down a corridor that smelled of ashes and rosewood, as in a funeral parlor. He walked in on a tall, thin-looking man of about forty. Chalmers, just then stretching, tilted back in a black leather easy chair. He saw in a corner, window office behind a desk covered with manuscripts, newspapers, and galley proofs.

"Come on in and have a seat."

Jon laid his manila envelope on the desk; or rather, on a foot-tall pile of assorted hardbound books. He and Chalmers shook hands and Jon sat down in an easy chair facing Ned Chalmers. The easy chair seemed to want to fling him into a semi-reclining attitude of relaxation. This wasn't suited to his elevated adrenal count in this emotional state. He sat on the edge of his chair while Chalmers picked up the envelope (a life's work in those surgically clean, lightly haired fingers!) and peered inside.

"I see...clippings...poems...nice..." Chalmers sat back and crossed his arms behind his head. The phone rang and he answered, "No, not yet... yes... maybe in five minutes... sure... naw, make mine with lox, cream cheese, no capers. Okay, see you in five." Chalmers again sat back. "Well, uh, Charles...hot outside, isn't it?"

Jon sank slowly back in the chair, realizing just how tiring had been his journey here—from New Haven, from a lifetime. Here he was, and the most pressing topic was a cream cheese bagel. He'd made this pilgrimage through dangerous, unfamiliar streets, through the pressing crowds of hundreds of thousands of people... "I'm glad I don't live in New York."

Chalmers chided gently, "Oh come on now."

Wrong start. I've already blown it. He hates me.

Chalmers was obviously just killing time until he could leave to eat his bagel. "I kind of enjoy it. My wife and I have a nice little apartment over in Brooklyn. This is one of the last places in America that has genuine old-fashioned neighborhood bars, you know. If you like to tip a beer once in a while, that is."

Jon thought of quiet New Haven neighborhoods where you could soak in the leafy, sunny solitude and write—poetry, the thing he'd come to peddle here, to fill the emptiness left by an absence of capers.

Chalmers grinned. "I see you are from New Haven. Must be nice there this time of year. I spent two years at Yale, then dropped out and went to Europe. The only thing I used to miss about New Haven when I was at Oxford were those long sandwiches, what do you call them?"

"Grinders," Jon informed him.

"Yes, sure," Chalmers remembered fondly. "They call them heroes here in New York." Chalmers, apparently unaware of Jon's desperate urgency, sat back, closed his eyes, and ruminated. "Yep. Maybe one of these days I'll get tired of big-city living and go back to Oregon."

Jon looked at the clock. Two minutes to bagel time. He gnawed at his lip. "About the poems, Mr. Chalmers... I was hoping you'd like them."

A frown briefly crossed the orbits of Chalmers' closed eyes. Then he smiled sadly. "I'm sorry," he said, sitting up. His blue eyes crinkled tiredly under bushy brown eyebrows and he ran a hand through his mussy, curly hair. "Sometimes I need to lean back and get in touch with myself. I do it at the oddest moments."

Jon said, "I'm sorry."

"That's okay," Chalmers said. "I know you've come a long way and you're anxious to present your work. So are a million others." He suddenly became quizzical. "What are the chances of a new fella like yourself getting into books? Slim, I'm afraid to say. Very slim."

Jon breathed, "Even if I'm very good?"

"Even if you are brilliantly gifted, which you might just be. Who knows. It's all about marketing." He regarded the pain on Jon's face. It didn't rattle him to see a man disintegrate emotionally—clearly, this was a common occurrence here. "It's supply and demand," Chalmers said. "We have too much supply and not enough demand."

So I'm dead.

Chalmers said generously, "Yet, there's always a chance. You have to stick with it. If you're lucky, you might just make it."

Luck. What the fuck?

"There is hope, then?" Jon asked. He'd forgotten all his carefully nurtured questions. He'd wanted to point out certain aspects of his syllabification and metrics, the breath, as Olson would have written, direct, *ex* Pound: He'd intended to prove that he had a theory. All his English classes failed him, even the many he hadn't bothered to attend because he was busy writing or thinking.

The atmosphere in Mr. Chalmers' office was less conducive to theory and more to sleep or to tepid tea.

"There is always hope," Chalmers reported with oracular mien. "Who are your favorite poets?"

An immense weight sank inside Jon. He looked past Chalmers' shoulder. It was a long, slow falling gaze, as if he were dropping through time and space and would eventually go splat on the sidewalk far below. He stared for a long time at the people gathered in the sunshine around the city library. They were all over it: The steps, the windows, the walls, the benches, the sidewalks, the grass...

Jon stared at that brightly clothed ant heap and wondered, *What am I trying to prove here? On whom am I trying to lay the freight and the weight of my poems? The weight that I'm alive that there are pretty young girls in New Haven, that I feel a union of heart and soul with the city, in all of its seasons and wondrous geography, from the baking boardwalk at Lighthouse Point in July to the oily sand near South Street beach in West Haven, to the gritty snow plowed by thousands of toothy truck tires on Orange Street in the winter, to the aching gray collapse of summer, to the jubilant flooding and tea-like steeping of St. Ronan Street in the spring...why should I export those precious wines to these sweaty spear carriers, money counters, and wearers of leather elbow patches?*

"Do you read a lot of poetry?" Chalmers asked patiently, a new hint of curiosity or alarm in his eyes as he stared close at Jon, who struggled to speak.

The clock has nearly run out. Bagels ahoy—a joy.

The feeling was momentary, however. Here he was, after all— finally—in the halls of a publisher, given an opportunity to speak. He saw now why they were all relaxed. This was everyday stuff to them; to him, Jon Harney, briefly escaped from the cliffed coral that was his life in New Haven, these were heady waters in which to swim. "Yes, I read a lot of poetry," he said. "I like..." and he enumerated until Chalmers laughed and held up a hand for peace. Chalmers said, "It's clear to me that you're well-read and I'm sure I'll enjoy reading your work. Can you give me a few weeks?"

"Sure." Jon was prepared to give him months if need be, as long as maybe a slender volume for the ages found its way into bookstores and classrooms and libraries. Was it possible that this man—whose single word could spell the difference between fame and namelessness for him—had just lowered himself to inquire of him, Jon Charles Egeny Harney, if he could have some time to read his poetry?

Yes, a thousand times yes. A real live publisher cares!

Chalmers rose, smiling, and held the door fully open. Jon took the hint, rose, and started out. Chalmers extended a broad, dry hand. He winked and said, "Good luck."

Good luck? What do you mean? It's in your hands.

Chalmers vanished into his office and Jon left as if buoyed by airbags. He felt a sudden fondness for the establishment of Mr. Eburgenhas. At the desk, the young woman smiled with white teeth, cherub skin, dangling bracelet, round breasts, violet eyes...

Feeling a thousand times lighter, Jon descended into the sweltering heat of the city. The manila folder with his hopes and theories and crafted phrases now lay in Mr. Chalmers' perceptive and sensitive hands, ready for a sympathetic reading. He beamed and fretted, threading his way among swarming humanity. Sure, he told himself. The poems would speak for themselves. They were passionate and rhythmical and jazzy. They'd justify his energy and hours at the typewriter, in the high garret, with the moths and the occasional silhouette stripper across the way.

It was late afternoon in the sweltering city. A pretzel vendor grinned with broad gold teeth. Two exotic young women in strapless dresses licked ice cream cones, pausing sensuously as a fire engine screamed past, its traffic horn booming between the high buildings. A jackhammer rattled amid yellow-black striped barricades. Nearby stood a young, slim, dark-haired cop with a knowing, sheepish grin and longish hair, directing a flock of nuns past an elderly lady defiantly curbing her ribboned poodle amid cardboard and garbage. Every ethnic group, every race, every nationality were represented, and in the blinding blistering heat, Jon wished he had a camera. But the pressing motion all around, super-heated, molecular, offering every conceivable diversion and danger, led him inexorably toward his escape point: the Port Authority Terminal. There, in a dark underground passage, were the buses that afforded departure. And there was only one thing he wanted to do just now: return to his typewriter, the way a dog returns to its dish. Charles Egeny had received some slight, enigmatic sustenance.

He dozed on the two-hour bus ride back to his city, bathed in a sense of fulfillment; back to the province, to the backwater where his all and his only and his truth reposed. As he dozed, he dreamed of Jane and Alice, who smiled whitely and with café-au-lait skin through braces; and he longed to pick up the phone and dial for Andy, to hear a familiar voice, to relish the timeless beery smell of places like the 7 Winds where time stood still and all things were as uncomplicated as a hot dog at a cookout...

His hands were relieved and empty now, for his sweaty envelope was in New York where everybody jostled. How could one stop to think in such a place? Logic dictated that truth lay in the hedges and mowed lawns of quiet old New Haven.

He woke, sweating despite the air-conditioning in the bus, and saw that they were traveling between green, leafy trees and they were now safely across the border on smooth Connecticut roads.

He dozed again, dreaming of bookstores, of Charles Egeny and autographs, dreams in which one of those rambling old wood houses with cool interiors was entirely his—and that of a perfect woman as yet unknown who would be perfect and fill his life.

His journey might have been measured in light years and astronomies. Now he reentered the sleepy, familiar city which was just then steeped in its pre-twilight exhaustion. It was an evening to start off right—by seeing his parents—he decided as he descended stiffly but with rested eyes and resurgent mind onto the familiar sidewalk. Somebody Italian was engaged in a vociferous argument with a Negro bus company official. A familiar looking Connecticut Company bus (*Congress Avenue-West Haven*) labored past, discharging diesel fumes whose distinct essence he would recognize if it were shipped to him bottled in Singapore.

Charging out of the bus company lot, he remembered that people did not run red lights here, and came to an equally abrupt stop at the corner of Crown and Chapel. An authoritative glare by a policeman in blue uniform served to dampen his fervor; but no matter, he'd have all night to discharge his job at being back, though he'd only been gone half a day.

Chapter 14

On a hot Saturday afternoon in early July, the telephone slumbered electronically under the rubber palm.

Merile, feeling feverish and cold despite the heat, lay on the couch wrapped in a sheet. The end table was sticky with spilt juice and crowded with the remains of conflicting drinks: stale coffee in a stained cup; flat cola in a warm glass; curdling milk in a small pitcher. She'd been having cramps all day and couldn't hold anything down. She'd been dozing fitfully and every noise—the children outside, the doors in the hallway, a radio next door—jabbed her like a knife. She'd turned on the TV and the oscillating fan, and thus shrouded herself in a veil of familiar noise. She woke only whenever one of the contestants on The Price is Right shrieked or a commercial babbled too loudly.

She awoke and it was dark. Startled, she sat up to see what time it was. It was eight and Bill hadn't called yet. Why? Groaning, she resolved to pass more time sleeping. The night air was chilly, and the humming fan bothered her. The television set resounded with the fanfare of some ponderous biblical bromide. Annoyed, she threw the sheet aside and turned fan and TV off. In the ensuing calm, she tried to nestle back into sleep. But she couldn't because she was sick and angry and disappointed. A dog barked someplace. An ice cream truck patrolled the dark streets with ringing bells under the moth-dancing lights. Somewhere, the stereo appropriate to a party blared cheap, pointless rock music.

She tossed her sheet aside, held her head in both hands, and forced herself to sit up. Dazed, she stared at the blank TV screen, realizing that the noise was not going to abate and that she might as well get up. Perhaps fix herself something to eat.

At nine-thirty the phone rang.

She was watching the last half of Trumpets in Galilee where an actor resembling Charlton Heston, as a captured renegade slave, sweated mightily from a long, handsome face (he even groaned huskily) while a huge, bald-headed overseer weighing 300 pounds whipped him, and a curly-haired man in a papier-mâché helmet laughed cruelly.

She answered the phone in a quiet, nerveless voice.

"Long distance, station to station from Australia. A Mr. Bill Doherty. Will you accept the charges?"

"Yes." She clenched her fist.

"Go ahead," said the operator, and in the same moment she heard Bill's voice. "Merile?"

"Yes. Are you all right?"

His voice was slightly slurry. He said brightly, "I'm sorry I'm calling late tonight. We're in Sydney at a party. Got caught in traffic and didn't make it here until half an hour ago."

"I was worried when you didn't call. I'm not feeling well today."

"Anything the matter?" As he spoke, she heard men and women laughing, music, a distant car horn.

"Just my period, I imagine. What are you doing there in Sidney? Or with Sidney?"

He sounded perhaps a shade too jocose. "Oh, we drifted up this way for the weekend. Brought along a crate of bones, potsherds, some ten-thousand-year-old egg shells. We're going to get some expert opinions."

Going to get laid, she thought to her herself, *but oh well what I don't know won't hurt me.* "How's the party?" She tried to couch her question in *ennui* rather than reveal a sharp edge of momentary jealousy.

He laughed, probably swaying slightly, for the phone rustled with some small struggle. "Oh…after all these weeks up on the coast, it's hellacious seeing civilization again—you know, streets, street lights, cars other than muddy Land Rovers—you know, things we take for granted back there."

She added, "I bet the girls are pretty too."

He said, "They are always pretty." He finished the sentence with a sigh, beginning to sound uncomfortable.

She resolved not to probe any further. She had feared it would be like this. She felt uncomfortable.

He said after a pause, "I wish you were here." He didn't sound sincere. He amended, "I wish I were there." That sounded fully sincere.

I'm glad I am here and you are there.

She told him, "Your parents are fine. They say hello."

With a spark of familiar interest suddenly kindled, he asked, "Do you get over to Fairfield County much?"

"Just about every Sunday," she said. She tried to find points of particular interest to relate out of the every day. She randomly enumerated, "Your father's gained a little weight. Your mother made an appointment for your brother's kids at a photographer's studio…"

"What's King up to?" he inquired fondly of his older brother, who owned a well-to-do real estate firm.

She started to reply, "He's doing very well. Why only two weeks ago he and Marie were…" She broke off when she heard a muffled, sinuous giggle; the phone rustled again. Merile felt distracted and found herself saying sharply, "Well, so much for expert opinion."

Her meaning was clear. He understood the accusation. "Really, Merile, it's nothing. You know how people at parties get. Everyone's been drinking…"

She overrode him with chatter designed to drown out the unpleasantness. Her voice, though pleasant, had a direct and purposeful edge to it. "So as I was saying, King and Marie were over at the Yale Medical Center because Marie is having that trouble again, you know, with the veins in her legs, and they stopped by for a few hours with little Johnny. He's quite a little rascal. He pulled all your ties down out of the closet. And a friend of yours stopped by, a Mister whatsisname, Charley Anderson from the Department."

Bill interrupted, "I don't…oh, yeah, I remember him, sort of a mealy-mouthed fellow…"

"I threw him out," she told him, smiling closely, almost giggling. The idea of Bill wondering about a little creep like this Anderson assuaged her sense of justice.

"What did he do?" Bill asked sharply.

"Nothing at all," she told him, settling back on the couch with purposeful, cat-like enjoyment as she toyed with him.

He never had a chance.

"He stopped off with some papers—he regularly drops off all sorts of mail sent to you at your office—this time he decided to come personally and bring all the information—and—well, I began to feel a bit funny about having him right here in the living room, you know...he got a little bit fresh, and I landed him on his ear."

Bill's voice was close and angry. "You keep that bum out of there. Besides, I told you not to have any strangers in the house."

You like to control things. For my safety, you said.

Enjoying herself, she turned on her back and crossed her left ankle over her right knee, swinging the phone cord by the side of the couch. She said, "I didn't want to be too hard on him. After all, he's assistant department chair."

Bill slurped quickly at a drink and said, "Never mind. I don't care if he's the Pope. I..." Bright, drunken, cascading, malicious feminine laughter interrupted. In the background, a canned orchestra played *Strangers in the Night*. She smiled grimly and thought:

Stranglers in the Night.

She goaded purposefully, looking for a reaction. Mainly, did Bill know about her lover? She said, "He was concerned about us."

She heard him curse.

She added, "About me. And about your career, since I'm such a loose strumpet here in this apartment."

He said, "We'll talk again. I've got to go. I don't like the atmosphere here. Keep that crawling crud out of the apartment. And ah, well, take care of yourself, and—dammit!"

Merile, abruptly losing interest in goading him, sat up. With a wry face, she said in her best voice, "Don't let me get between you and your party."

He sounded harried. "Oh for heaven's sake, Merile, goodbye. I love you. Goodbye."

She sensed that he was waiting impatiently for her to let him sign off from his obligatory call. Still, she felt shocked. This wasn't real.

She whispered, "Love you. Goodbye," and let the receiver fall gently onto its cradle.

Alone again, she whirled, crossed her arms, and buried her face into the pillow under the rubber palm. Her shoulders heaved.

Chapter 15

It was nighttime, but the heat still moved in muggy sheets over the Sound off West Haven. Fog horns in all sorts of high and low tones moaned in the night as ships talked to one another on the shipping lanes, to avoid colliding or running aground.

Andy, toweling his curly hair and sputtering with his round face, entered the screened-in back porch where Jon sat reading. Jon looked up and said, "I've been counting the moths hitting the screen."

"We'll go dig up some excitement," Andy promised, sitting down heavily at the card table. He threw the towel down. "What a hot night!"

Jon tossed the magazine aside and reclined on the couch. They'd been swimming that afternoon. Jon had gone to his parents' house to shower and eat supper, then he'd come to Andy's parents' house. Dawn and their parents had gone to a movie. Jon said, "I don't know if I could ever live in West Haven again. I remember when we were in high school and had to hitchhike everywhere."

Andy rubbed his shaven cheeks thoughtfully, staring vacantly in the yellowish porch light. "Can't go back," he said. He quickened, "Besides, we're not in school anymore. We have cars now, and no one tells us when to be home."

The tang of Andy's aftershave awakened in Jon the impulse to go hunting for women, a primordial preoccupation of young men bred in the suburbs. He rose and tapped out a two-handed tom-tom on his navel. "Ready to go?"

Ten minutes later, Andy had locked up the house and left a note. They chose to drive in Jon's car.

Half an hour later as they parked on a side street in downtown New Haven, Andy said, "I'm getting so I could walk this stretch blindfolded."

"The routine does grow on one," Jon observed as they strode into the air-conditioned coolness of their favorite student bar, the Kino Café.

They sat crowded in a corner at a windowsill. The place swarmed with a blue-jeans and long-hair crowd. Rock music blared from speakers in each corner. "Not too many girls," Andy said, looking hungrily about.

"I must be getting old," Jon said, shaking his head at the sight of a pair of pert young things holding brews. College girls, they wore mechanics' overalls over preppy pink T-shirts. They had glowing baby cheeks and carefully silken hair, and engaged in admiring conversation with a ratty-looking group of local musician heroes.

"We just don't suit the image," Andy agreed.

"Where do we fit in?" Jon questioned. He held up his newly arrived, pearly-beaded bottle of Black Horse Ale. They clicked bottles and quaffed thirstily.

"Ah! That hits the spot!" Andy gasped, wiping foam from his nose.

Jon grinned. "Another night on the prowl."

Andy shrugged lightly. "The hunt is sort of fun in itself as long as there's cold ale to be had, if no hot babes."

Feeling out of place, being neither nineteen nor ratty-looking musicians, they sat quietly and observed the welter of human activity.

"It's the pairing instinct," Andy remarked.

"The mating drive," Jon agreed.

"The king crabs ought to be down on the beach pretty soon. It's the first week in August."

"Yes," Jon said, "and summer is almost over."

Andy looked startled and briefly glum at this realization. Then he brightened, "If we were king crabs we'd have it made."

Jon laughed. "Unless we were twenty-four year-old king crabs. That's probably old for a king crab."

Andy said, "After zillions of years of evolution, if we were king crabs, we'd probably be hanging around just like we are now, but on a beach, looking for chick crabs or queen crabs."

"Or catching crabs."

Andy looked fated. "I think we were made for this."

They were silent, reflecting on the annual convergence of thousands of huge horseshoe crabs on Connecticut beaches during hot August nights—silent, enigmatic armored aliens, whose razor-sharp pointed tails could pierce a bare foot taking a false step on night sand.

Andy drained his bottle with a definitive gasp, clapping it down on the table. "We may be king crabs, but won't find any queen crabs here. Maybe queer crabs."

"Let's go."

It seemed every soul who could had found an air conditioner to sit by. The streets were empty. Signal lights changed colors in lone and steady rhythm.

They walked aimlessly around the fringes of Yale's neo-Gothic architecture. "Dead," Andy judged. "Another dead night in New Haven."

Jon said nothing of his tiring foray into New York. It was not a night for Charles Egeny; the hunt itself, vestige of teenage years, those first-car years, prowling the beachside suburbs, promised more excitement. In the coolness after midnight, perhaps, Charles Egeny might drive his neighbors crazy with typing. Not now. Life was to be lived.

Andy—professional bartender educated as a philosopher— suggested, "We could take a ride down toward Westport." Fairfield County was a wealthy bedroom suburb of all the money and fame in Manhattan; home of Merile and Bill Doherty and their banks.

Jon shrugged. "No more Alices, thank you."

Andy snapped his finger. "Look, how about Guilford and Madison?" More beach towns, but east toward Rhode Island.

Jon spread his hands. "Why not?" Enthused, they headed toward the car.

Andy lay back morosely as Jon drove on I-95. Vistas of brightly lit towns alternated with muggy seascapes and the wind rustled coolly in the open car. They had to stop at a gas station to put the top up. This was not a refreshing breeze. Hot, soupy night air combed into their hair a stickiness like tallow. The only good thing was that maybe at sixty or faster, you could outrun ubiquitous, whining, voraciously gnawing mosquitoes.

Once they were out of the suburbs of New Haven, riding through avenues of shadowy forest, the air seemed to acquire some redeeming touch of coolness. Andy sat up with renewed energy. "We do this summer after summer."

"Do what?" Jon asked, combing his hair with one hand while he drove.

Andy stared out into the darkness. "Maybe if we had decent jobs," he muttered.

"Cheer up," Jon said. "The Guilford Marina's full of material."

Andy broke into a smile. "Yeah." He lay back again, letting the night wind cool his face.

The steady movement of red taillights became swallowed up by the increasing brightness of streetlights as they approached Guilford. The landscape was all lights: canneries, warehouses, homes…then the sea.

As they drove through the quiet town streets, they saw the strung lights of the marina ahead.

"Wow," said Andy as they pulled into the parking lot of the marina complex. Restaurants, boutiques, bars, and arcades thronged with casually walking people beckoned—a come-on for tourists and single men on the prowl. On a wooden railing sat the teenage members of a motorcycle group, smoking cigarettes and engaged in their own mating ritual. Myriad lights glittered on the water. Dozens of boats, ranging from small cabin cruisers to long white yachts, were moored under thousands of tiny, colorful pennants—their own gang colors, like those of bikers but with money. Clashing energies (but matching rhythms) of rock bands in two separate night spots urgently massaged the night air around Jon and Andy like a giant mating dance. *King crabs indeed*, Jon thought. Aromas of French fry grease and sea food mingled in the air with perfume and motor oil. They leaned for a while against the railing on top of the sea wall and watched feminine bodies swaying past.

"Not too many single girls," Andy reported after squinting silently up and down the wharf. Not the first time, it sounded the death knell to a night of girl hunting.

Jon suggested, "Let's go have a drink."

"How much money do you have?" Andy asked, pulling out his wallet.

"Fifteen bucks," Jon said.

"Twenty bucks," Andy reported. "We'll really go far."

Jon laughed. "Maybe we'll get invited onto a yacht." He pronounced it *ee-awtcht*.

"Lotta money here," Andy said as they sidled through the entrance corridor of a nightclub. The throb of rock music and the smells of perfume, carpets, and sweet-sharp liquor greeted them, mellowing the pain of paying a $3 admission fee to a shadowy figure in a tuxedo.

Jon felt giddy and electrified.

Deep carpeting under his feet; a refreshing sea wind, full of kelp and salt, penetrated the air-conditioned interior that glowed red and amber. Glittering bodies gyrated under strobe lights while pounding rock music throbbed through their bones. Ice tinkled in glasses.

Here there be buttocks and pear-breasts, in white deck pants revealing the outlines of (if worn) briefs hulling poignant pink skin.

Jon stood transfixed at the sight of a young lady with sugary skin and shag-cut black hair and coal Italic eyes and sharp features, dancing with an accountant in a Madras suit, while Andy fetched two drinks. The young lady was skinny, and she held up thin arms while bobbing avid buttocks, and each motion of her bottom caused the loose front of her backless jersey to shift, revealing small, round, bouncing breasts like caramel ice cream scoops.

Andy pushed his way through the onlookers. "Ouch—three bucks apiece," he lamented, while thrusting an icy Scotch-and-water into Jon's hand.

Jon accepted the drink and glared at his friend. "We have enough money to get drunk, if nothing else."

"I want to meet a heavenly girl," Andy protested.

"I don't think you will here either," Jon said.

"We could have stayed in the city and drunk a gallon of beer."

"You're gross," Jon told him.

"What's so gross about our favorite ale?"

Jon had to admit wryly, nothing was wrong with their main venues along Chapel Street. To say anything was wrong with the sacramental beer would have been like a lewd comment about, oh well.

Andy inveigled himself toward the end of the bar, where he sought and accepted the charms of a female of the species with frosted hair, who instantly understood his hunger and let Andy put a hand on her rear end. As Jon watched, Andy and the woman danced briefly. Jon turned away to look longingly after a young girl with auburn curls and a smooth body verging on ripeness, who was engaged in a rollicking tango with a smooth, dark-haired young man in a puffy white blouse. Andy and the frosted, aging bar fly parted company. She had mistaken him for having money, and he was disappointed by the sharp, hungry lines around her mouth and eyes. It was a cruel world in this reddish light, this amber sea with its dusky food chain—predators, bottom feeders, and drifting krill.

Jon was summoning his courage to approach a pouting young debutante in a long red gown, when the sight of a group at a far table deflated his courage abruptly. He seized Andy's arm.

"What's the matter with you?" said Andy, new from his disappointment. Jon pointed with his chin. At that far table, which showed evidence of having had a sumptuous dinner upon it, were two men and three women. One of the men was a tall, fiftyish gentleman with a tanned, seamed face and bald head. The second man was short, pudgy, smiling figure with a dark goatee. The two elder women were pressed together, laughing at some joke being told by the tall, bald man. The third woman, tall, blonde, and with a narrow attractive yacht club face, sat in the shadows as if only half there, a ghostly presence who merely smiled downward, alone, staring into some thousand-yard tragic vision. She did not seem to have seen Jon.

"That's her," Jon whispered to Andy.

You almost don't even look like you. Is that loving feeling gone, gone, gone already?

"Who?" Andy demanded, prying his arm free.

"The one I was going with," Jon said.

Andy stared across the sweaty, pulsatiously lit dance floor. "Wow, she really is a looker. You had a good thing there."

"Do you mind if we leave?" Jon said.

Andy put aside his glass, whose dross of melting ice slivers and watery scotch he had been nursing. "Anything you say."

Minutes later, they stood inhaling ocean and kelp smells from above the sea wall. Fragments of laughter and rock music reached them from the nightclub they had abruptly left. Andy leaned back and inhaled the pretty air deeply. "Ahh…it's good to be alive. Someday, you know, we're both going to have a piece of all this perfume and good looks."

Jon gripped the railing and stared out over the twinkling water, toward a jetty with a distantly winking garnet-red alarm light.

Andy turned and gripped the railing beside him. His face bore a wistful smile. "Maybe not this summer."

Jon shook his head. "I already have."

Charles Egeny. Harbor lights.

Chapter 16

It was far past midnight, too late for ice cream trucks or children or cruising taxis. An insect, some night predator, hunted in the waxy leaves of the rubber palm. Finding a victim, it stung deeply and sure, settling with hair-fine legs onto its dying prey.

Cool night air probed through darkness. Snoring fitfully, sprawled under shadowy sheets, she dreamed: Bones; desk drawers; Westport; floating men smiling; horror grimaces; mud—she searched frantically, paranoically, for a testament sunk in a green pond.

The air was ringing.

The telephone, startled under its rubber tree, agonized with long ringing. Groans and protests in the night attested to its disturbing effects. Eventually, there was a gasp in the bedroom. With a rustling amid bedsheets, a woman moved, placing sweaty palms on the bed beside her, placing damp soles on the wood floor. The call of the telephone was unrelenting.

"I'm coming..." she mumbled, staggering through the darkness, fumbling with the receiver.

"Night call, station to station from Australia, a Mr. Bill Doherty, will you accept...?"

"Yes, yes, put him on."

He sounded close by. "Merile, did I wake you? I'm worried."

I was just dreaming that I was diving for you deep in the sea, and you were nowhere to be found.

"I'm sorry," he said. "I'm sorry about everything. I was trying to reach you all evening.

She drew her fingers through her hair and said in a muffled voice, "What—what time is it?"

"It's seven p.m.," he said.

Three a.m. here. Always your time zone, never mine.

"Look, should I call you back in the morning?"

"No," she told him, "go ahead." The pained, distant quality in his voice was unmistakable. They had a good connection and every fibrous rustle, every labor of his breath was distinct.

"Merile…Oh hell, I can't stand it any longer. Look, it's about us. There is nothing for us. Nothing. I just can't go on with this charade. I've been away all this time and…"

She weaved in the darkness, trying to unzip the back of her little black dress. "It's three in the morning," she said.

"You've been out, haven't you?" he accused.

She laughed, smelling lemon and gin on herself. "I've been out, I've been out; yes, I've been out—why should I sit here by myself?"

His voice was cold and distinct. "Why should we pretend anymore? It's all over. I can't stand it any longer."

She sing-songed, "It's all over, it's all over, oh so over."

"You're drunk," he said.

She leaned dangerously on the arm of the couch. "I am not," she said. "Walk the line, touch my nose. Don't fall down. One two three four, three two one, I'm wide awake."

His voice was crisp and indignant. "Hear me out. Merile, I've fallen in love. Oh, I wasn't looking for it. I've been out in the sticks too long. Suddenly this angel came along. I saw things clearly. We haven't got a thing going for us over there. I hate to tell you—I feel free for the first time in many years. Her name is Madelaine and…"

"Madelaine!" she said. "What a pretty name. I'll bet she's French. *Parlez-vouz a-humma-humma?*"

"Go ahead," he told her. "I deserve it, I suppose. Oh, Merile, I've tried, all this time…"

"I've tried, I've tried," she sang tunelessly, swaying on the edge of the couch. That zipper—so important—there; she had it open, and rose. Her dress fell down around her feet.

"Merile, I'm sorry."

She undid her bra and threw it across the room.

"Merile, I do love you—but this isn't the same."

She stepped out of her panties and threw them across the room.

"Merile, I'm putting everything on the line. It's over between us. You know all those…problems of mine? I feel like they're a dream. Finally, I feel whole and together. Oh dammit, say something."

She said, "Why because you found some dried up desert—I should—well no, the hell with you—please, tell me, she's French isn't she? Does she do it better…"

"Merile, for the last time. Please."

"Please what? What please?" she parodied. "Say something, Merile, please."

You need me to say it's okay, you spineless, needy bastard. It's not and I won't. You don't deserve that much.

"Merile…I am trying hard here…"

"Master Doherty," she said. "Master Doherty, I'm drunk and I don't care but I have been waiting—oh I have been waiting. I held your cigar, but I'm afraid your flame has gone out. It's an exploding cigar, a joke, I fear. What do you mean asking me please at three in the morning Huh? Answer me that. At three in the morning. I'm sleeping, you hear? It's early there and you are going out to screw your Madelaine and I am going back to sleep because I've had too many gin and tonics. I am all alone here. My, how time flies. When you're having a good time. What a wonderful way to pass the time."

He rustled uncomfortably. "Merile, I'll call you again. We're always honest with each other, right?"

Ha! Creep!

He said, "I couldn't hold it in any longer."

She sat down hard on the couch, her nakedness tingling against the brushing material. "So long, Master Doherty. Fare thee well." She had mastered the art of crying and laughing all at once. Tears dribbled on the receiver, laughing, until she choked with sorrow.

"I'll call you tomorrow," he lied.

She dropped the receiver rattling into its cradle under the rubber palm. She crouched down and cried loudly, framed by darkness. Her shoulders shook—not from laughing. Brokenhearted, she wailed like a child amid unimaginably cruel tragedy. She cried for the lost years, and her pretty eyes, and all the times she'd gone to bed alone.

Chapter 17

The stairway smelled of cat. He knocked hesitantly, then stood back in semidarkness, sweating in the heat. The door opened a crack. Blue eyes blinked.

"Taxi," he said.

The door opened wide and there stood Merile, tall and surprised.

Timing and tragedy; that's no strategy; but it makes for beautiful drama.

He said, "Did you call for a taxi?"

She tossed her blonde hair. He saw she had the beginning of lines in the corners of her eyes and mouth, but only if you looked closely. She might look twenty-three, in a blur, if you stayed moving.

They regarded each other frankly.

"Come in."

He trod across the lacquered floor. "Is this the right address? Are you Madame Canary, and did you call for assistance?"

She laughed and closed the door behind him and leaned against it. "How have you been?"

Jon turned and regarded her. "I saw you a couple of days ago in Guilford."

She grinned and wrinkled her nose. "I was out."

He put his hands in his pockets, surveying the apartment. "Just wondering. Thought I might stop by and see how you are."

"Who is Madame Canary?"

"Some blonde who stole my taxi and has the meter running. She took my heart with her as well."

She looked deeply pleased and amused as she took him by the hand and led him to the couch. "How about a glass of juice?"

"I will if you will."

As she bustled brightly into the kitchen, he helicoptered a hand ambivalently over the couch beside him.

Does she still want me—as much as I want her?

She called from the kitchen, from amid a tinkling of ice cubes and their rattle in a plastic pitcher, "How is Charles Egeny doing?"

Surprised, he said, "Oh…waiting as always." He mentioned the publishing house of Eburgenhas.

She marched briskly into the living room bearing a tall glass beaded with cold droplets. She sat down directly beside him. "That makes two of us."

He accepted the glass. "Thank you."

Summer was nearly over. Powerful New England fall came pounding at the doors of the heart.

He sipped at the raspberry liquid. "What have you been up to?"

She gathered her house dress at the knees and breathed back coolly, "Waiting."

"That's it?"

All the money, beauty, power, sunlight trapped in glass tabletops, brutality…

She shrugged helplessly, with her elbows on her knees and her bare, tanned arms wrapped around her elegant body. "What else is there?"

There is nothing if there isn't you.

Part Three: Fall

Chapter 18

It's called autumn elsewhere—but fall in New England. You could not mistake that skipped heartbeat every New Englander unexpectedly feels at some random moment in late August. Men and women boating under bright sails on Long Island suddenly pause, look up at a ghostly change sweeping across the sun, the sky, like a dimming of light, an extinction of youth and hope, a drowning of poems in chilly and fishy brine. A gadzillion trees feel it and tremble, whispering to each other as their leaves prepare to die. Fall is marching down from Canada, the frost line, so many miles a day, time to turn out the lights and go to bed for the winter. Days are growing shorter, nights longer...

The dying breaths of the season of long days are called Indian summer. It is the last burst, even as fall sets in. It is the glory of football weather, when people wear sweaters on sunny days as they fill the bleachers at ball games. It is spring in reverse for leaves and other leaving things. The weather is mild, conquered, native, memorious as Borges' Ireneo Funes; a dying Persephone promising rebirth to come in the next Neolithic growing cycle...

For three golden-yellow days the heat and haze had beaten down on New Haven. The Sound was covered with white, red, and blue sails nudging through rationed space. But the fall message penetrated every nook and cranny of hope and desire. As Rilke wrote while wandering the boulevards of his city, *Who by now does not already have a house, he will never build one...*

Top down and radio rocking, the Pontiac Firebird churned on hot tires along the miles of I-95 headed toward Rhode Island, toward Cape Cod. Jon had found a job driving a taxi around the New Haven area; dangerous work, not for the long term. One needed to think of how to fly one's jet over the horizon where clouds and future years hung, stacked for inevitable and wondrous passage.

"I'm sort of surprised," Merile said, tying a bandana around her blonde hair. Hot, dying wind blew around her handsomely, tragically beautiful face.

"Why is that?" cried Jon Harney, alias Charles Egeny, through the rattling wind making a shell over the open-top convertible. He felt beach grit under his bare feet, and his under-thighs were stuck sweatily to the plastic seat.

"You don't fit the image," she said smugly.

"I'm not sure I understand," he cried, extending his left arm out of the car, with hand moving up and down in sinuous motions like an airplane wing.

She snuggled over and laid both hands on him, planting a kiss on his upper arm just below the hem of his T-shirt. "I mean, you're supposed to be spoiled rich and just out of Harvard, riding along in Daddy's Morgan instead of this General Motors heap."

"I like my goddam car!" He patted its sticky plastic seat with hard slapping motions.

She snuggled. "I do too."

"What are you talking about?"

She laughed and enjoyed her freedom. Her eyes stayed half-closed as she faced into beating sun and wind.

A while later they stopped for gas at a station just inside Rhode Island. Summer heat glowered oppressively, but the sea horizon was tinged with blue-black clouds like welts: first autumn storms.

"I think it will rain tonight," said a gas station attendant, wiping his sweaty forehead and peering through reddened eyes as he leaned on the gurgling pump. He leaned on the Firebird's sensuously rounded rear fender.

Merile had to use the ladies' room and Jon Harney waited by the cricket-haunted grasses, dangerous with poison ivy; and time stood still, until water flushed behind the white-tile walls and the battered door creaked open, emitting Merile, long tanned legs, short white dress, double-knit yellow sweater with round breast outlines, and flowing golden hair. Her face and hair dripped as she wiped away refreshing moisture with a paper towel. "I'm anxious to do private and moist things with you," Jon Harney told her as she returned to him. She submitted to his earnest confrontation, shying against white tiles. Smells of tar, tires, grass, and gasoline draped like sails all about in sticky heat. A faint wind idly moved the hem of her short white dress. She waited to hold his cigar, and he shared it in a totality of love. It was one thing she best understood and cherished—so her eyes and fingers told him across the differences.

If only... Si seulement...

* * * *

Soon again the tires hummed hot on tarry highways. Bug spatter crusted the windshield and choked the radiator.

By late afternoon they threaded through narrow Cape Cod streets choked with tourist cars. Evening came with a relenting coolness and dry lightning flashed over the sea as they found side streets outside Provincetown, which led them to a motel.

Thunder growled up through the rocks from the sea. She had withdrawn money earned by herself and Bill and gave it to Jon so he could pay. He showed his identification and used the checkbook in his name; the eye in the pyramid would be blind tonight. He finished the transaction with a bored clerk at a slatted customer service shack. He carried the cooler from his trunk to their room. Lightning flashed silently, eventually followed by growling distant thunder as a healing wind swept over the walkways on the ground floor overlooking the path down to the beach, the shell line, the tide line, the sea that stretched to the horizon and the galaxy beyond rising cloud forms.

Inside, he lay on his back and watched as she unpacked their clothes, wine bottle, and cooler from the trunk.

They hurried over concrete walkways in the motel compound just as the first broad, butter-warm droplets stained the hot cement.

Lightning flashed, and thunder smashed. Hail pounded on an exposed patio as Jon slid their aluminum-framed door shut. Merile, slender and poised and vanilla, bent over the cooler they had brought. She sorted through soda cans, plus their red wine bottle for later.

"Very domestic," he said.

"You like that," she said.

"Yeah. This could be eternity and we'd be in heaven."

"I could dig that." She added, "With you."

"You are so perfect."

"I wish. For you."

"And you?"

"I could hold your cigar."

"If I had one."

"You will."

"How do you know?"

"Because I love you."

"I adore you. So there."

"I'm just a secretary—smart, but not brilliant like you or Bill. I was going to be on a calendar of beautiful beach girls once, but he wouldn't let me."

"When?"

"Ten years ago."

"Why?"

"He needs to control."

Jon rolled his eyes up. "You go right now and be in that calendar." His heart ached for her lost chances.

She made a sweet, wistful face and said in a forlorn tone, "Too old. They want girls your age or younger."

"I would keep you forever."

"I'd love to be." She added, "Kept by you."

"Problem is I don't have a cigar and I have nothing to give you."

"You already are."

"No, I mean, as a man, to protect you, to shelter you, to build you a place out of mammoth tusks and keep out the sabertooth cats and other predators, including insecure faculty bullies."

"Worse yet," she said, "greasy little wannabes."

"We are safe here," he said.

"From the world," she whispered as she bent over to arrange things in the little fridge. "I like being your wife."

Mercurial rain drops encased them, sealing their time and space off like an aquarium. As she worked, Jon sat down in an easy chair near the cracked door and savored long-awaited coolness, a salty fresh breeze that ruffled stagnant curtains. He breathed an atmosphere of upholstery, carpets, cleaning agents—pretenses and hopes—while she bent over the cooler and removed items to place them inside the glowing refrigerator. In a dim light leaking from outside, dazzling refrigerator light x-rayed her white skirt. His eyes traced the tan contours of her thighs. With dangling hair and crook'd knees and waggling elbows, she concentrated on her work.

"Do you really think he doesn't suspect?" His voice quavered.

She closed the refrigerator, shutting off his voyeuristic movie, and came to sit on the armrest of his chair. He felt her knees against his leg and rested his hand on a round, firm buttock. As he did so he wondered if there was a mathematical equation which could render that curve, from the wealth of thigh through the amplitude of buttock to the abrupt hip bone and the frail waist where blood pounded under downy skin.

"No," she said intimately.

No, what? No bananas today, no show, no he doesn't.

"But he wouldn't care."

Jon was astonished. "The man who married you. Who made all kinds of promises. And you held his cigar."

"It was an exploding cigar. He was full of itching powder and made me sneeze."

"I care," Jon said meaning he cared about her.

"I don't care anymore." She bent down to press a kiss on his nose and her hands were cupped around his jaws. "Are you afraid?" She stroked his hair.

"No, I love you too much to care."

We are one soul. I want to cry—not for losing you, but to have you, keep you, cherish is the word.

She whispered, "This is our little space. Just you and me. You can keep me and be nice to me."

"I will."

She murmured. "Promise you will be sweet to me."

"I love you."

She lowered her voice to a broken whisper. "Promise you'll be tender and take care of me." She sat on his lap and stroked his hair until they kissed and he gently urged her onto her back. With her hands, she pulled on his shoulder blades to bring him down upon her. She was already breathing hard. Her eyes were half closed in a delirium of taking and letting go.

He fell into her galaxy and it was wondrous like a ride among suns. This would be their weekend together, alone and cut off from all external worldly thoughts, people, and concerns.

Just you and me.

It rained most of the time (of course) but they did walk on the beach, holding hands, and had hot chocolates in a seaside café and strolled through art galleries and made love (again and again) in the shadowy room with no clock.

You are so on my calendar.

Chapter 19

Jon closed his eyes and lay back in the easy chair on Merile's second-story back porch in New Haven. The mixed essences of lemon and skin cream and mowed lawns rose up into his nostrils. It was the first week in September, with Labor Day just passed, and fall officially just days away on the equinox of autumn—equilibrium, balance, when the scales of fate cancel each other in their fullness; harvest time since Stone Ages long ago. Time to harvest and lay in for winter, toiling under a full dark cheese moon bloodied on its rind; rich with time and truths that nobody can ever avoid.

A year ago, at Labor Day, he'd finished his last exams. He was not going to school this year, for the first time in many years. The loss was a felt one, and he resolved that the next Labor Day would find him enrolled for further liberal arts someplace. Or maybe law school, or anything. Labor Day was a learned reflex—he should not let another one go by with these mixed feelings of guilt and indolence.

"Honey, are you restless?" Merile said as if he were her husband and she his wife.

"Just thinking," he said.

"About what?" she said gently.

He opened his eyes and stared up into the trees. "I was just thinking about school."

She sighed. Thoughtfully, she folded her hands on her belly as if to tell him something. She started to—then paused, had second thoughts—and stretched silently instead. She wore a merlot bikini and her skin was tanned and glossy with sun lotion. "You really have to get away from that taxi-driving job," she told him. "I worry about you getting hurt. And do something more executive." She wrinkled her eyes calmly and lovingly. "You've got the stuff."

He stared sidelong down the side of his nose. "I don't know where to start or stop, just kiss every inch of you."

He relished the sight of her long, slender body with its ripe thighs and concupiscent navel. He told her, "I am so lost in you." He was thinking of how well he knew the grooves and smooth planes of her body. She was like a long-playing LP and he could play her, quietly, like a lengthy symphony, in the dark while resting his head in her arm and lying beside her. They could breathe the same air and grow drowsy together.

"You're just saying that," she said, self-consciously folding her hands together. She gave him a yank. "Keep saying that."

They laughed.

He ached for every curve and every pore of her. Yet he was not happy. Desperately, Charles Egeny—who could not compose in half-truths—yearned to find independence and a more perfect union. He had not written a poem since he'd spotted her melancholic smile in the salty and perfumed air of the *ee-yatcht* club in Guilford. She was nearly thirty and it made him want to vault over the porch, to leave her and seek the true tan flesh which would spell hope to his demanding sense of—oh Charles Egeny, you would not die of old age without once more partaking more permanently of young skin wet with aspiration. In other words, you will want to seek a younger chick. Such moments came and went—a song played on both their gramophones at once, and they each knew it. The brevity of their wonder together made it all the more wonderful.

The phone under the rubber palm rang stridently, and she slowly moved her lithe body to answer.

Jon regarded the elm leaves beyond the porch with alarm, hearing the bitter and matter-of-fact sound of her voice in the living room. He was preoccupied with the feeling of Charles Egeny, that surely there must be some youthful and spoiling skin, Alice or her sister, prepared to homage the dream of the green pond—for surely why this again women from Westport disappointed and used when surely there were quadrillions of young vestals awaiting the chance of Charles Egeny's expertise in the consuming fire of love and passion?

When she returned from the living room, he felt a sinking sensation occasioned by her downcast eyes.

"That was Bill," she said, settling back into her chair.

He sat upright and tried to fathom her worried facial lines as she straddled the easy chair in sitting down.

She said, "He is coming home on leave. For a month. He is going to ask for a divorce."

Jon settled back in the chair. "You going to fight it?"

Her fine face, irradiated with acceptance, was clever and weary and lined. "No, I won't," she said almost absently or maybe defeatedly.

"Not on account of me," he said.

She looked pained. "Of course not." She smiled at her lover the poet Charles Egeny. He regarded her anxiously.

She said, "Don't worry."

He lay back. Heat streamed around his eyes.

She said, "Oh, Jon. I know you are looking."

He lay back, hands folded on his flat stomach, pretending ignorance.

She said, "I know you aren't looking just now, but you will be looking for someone your own age."

He felt pained. "Do you know how beautiful you are?"

She said sadly, "I'm not the love you are looking for."

He sat up in denial, knowing he was lying. "I could hold on to you as long as I live."

She reclined. Her breasts, in their diminutive sheath, puckered. She said, "I wish."

"It's all about wishing, and hoping, like in the song." He rose and went to sit beside her. He lifted her hand to his mouth, noting how carefully her fingernails were trimmed and how fragrant were her knuckles.

She looked up at him. "I won't be able to see you the whole month he is here."

He kissed her hand, drawing her to him. She rose, girlish and graceful, firm in that mature, intriguing, ripe way, forbidden fruit. She padded after him into the bedroom where he kissed her, pressing her panties down along her thighs as he pressed his mouth to hers and her tongue stabbed around wetly seeking his tongue.

She let him do what he wanted. He was sweet and passionate and gentle but strong.

She helped eagerly, welcoming his firm command of her. She gave herself to him, pleading with her eyes and expression to take her, and take her more, anything at all.

Afterward, when they lay in the sweaty, ripped bed together, she pressed her thighs against his. She whispered, "Tell me again. Do you really think I am beautiful?" She curled up in a fetal position by his side. Her hair obscured his view of her eyes, revealing only the horizon of her forehead as he looked down and pulled her close.

He was naked; his hair was plastered to his forehead, and he moved lazily in the cooling night. His answer was exhausted, heavy, and truthful. "Yes."

He embraced her like the friend and love she was, and she snuggled like a kitten against him.

They rubbed noses and talked in little pretty noises, cooing and coaxing and laughing together to bring each other yet more pleasure and love. Her eyes glowed, seeking his with her gaze, while she framed his face between her hands.

He planted a little kiss slowly moving across her forehead. She murmured or mewled with her eyes closed, burrowing closer to him; and pressed her face to his chest.

Chapter 20

Autumn: Edgerton Park: A magnificent bequest to the city and the people of New Haven by a long dead oligarch; but no dogs or ball-playing allowed. Charles Egeny wandered the grounds with pen and notebook in his pocket, seeking to distill poesy or pick poesies wherever butterflies chanced upon a late, burnished cord or chord of sunlight.

Late-afternoon haze of a hot Indian summer day in fall curried through the blown grass of the many-acred estate. The devastating final bequest had required razing the Brewster family's stately early twentieth century mansion. Now only grassy, dazed acreage slept amid concrete walks and poison ivy, and a broad fountain among disused carriage paths. A glassy greenhouse still harbored exotic plants, hidden in a copse of elm trees. In a hidden, faux river bed between wind-blown banks, a small stone bridge spanned grassland and forest. There might have been the suspenseful silence of Versailles or Würzburg—instead, only the late-summer heat crawled around the filled-in cellars of the demolished and deported mansion.

Oblivious of laws, a golden-maned spaniel fetched sticks on the estate's rolling lawns. A grinning man on a bicycle pedaled furiously on a crumbling carriage path as Charles Egeny sat with his back against a tree and replucked triadic chords on his poetic kythara.

It's life, and life must go on until it doesn't, and by turns glorious and terrifying (like lightning flashes) while it does; but that is the wonder and the thunder of it.

It was still summer, after a fashion, when Jon parked his car outside the park's brown stone walls. He entered the park by its rustling gravel walk, mindful in a dim way that once Eli Whitney no doubt walked the same ground pondering his cotton gin and mass-manufactured rifles. Over some hills, nestled in slums on Winchester Avenue, lay a massive factory whose guns defeated Custer.

He found Merile sitting on a bench in the graying atmosphere amid a closure of pine trees in a corner of the great estate. She wore a short, black cotton dress. Her hands were curled together over her groin. Her tan neck was declined. Her blonde hair was bound up in a bun, and her fine nose, blue eyes, and elegant tannin-bronzed cheeks were declined upon an earth blanket of browned pine needles. He ran toward her, bounding over compressed moss and pine needles. Trucks roared past on Whitney Avenue outside as he took her in his arms. They walked arm in arm on a hard clay path where birds warbled wetly and crickets shrilled amid poison ivy and unkempt grass.

"I came as soon as I got your message," he said.

She clung to his arm. "It's true, what I was afraid of."

Like a hammering fist, defeat pounded down on his head. The if-only and had-I-buts multiplied like swarming bees as he fought off a bout of giddiness. Senselessly he wondered about the middle ages. Could Farmer F claim a turnip grown upon the land of Farmer G, if it was the lawful and cognizant land of G, whatever that meant, but unlawfully and cognizantly made fertile by the hand of F, upon realizing that it was patently likely that this acre of tillage would lie fallow under the careless hand of G? A turnip was a turnip. Who should eat it? Or should the earth above it be tamped and poisoned to obviate its burgeoning reality? Was it a turnip at all until its green shoots pierced the earth, became leaves, and soaked in sunlight?

She stopped and placed a hand on his cheek. He stared at her helplessly and with anguish. She said, "Let me take care of it. You didn't know. I should have taken precautions. Don't let me cloud your life with my stupidity. I don't want you to remember me with pain."

He thrust his hands in his pockets. "I can't run from this."

"Nobody is asking you. This is not your situation. Not really. Is it? If he were a real husband?" She smiled through her tears. "What would you do? Marry me? I'm still married to Bill. He's been back for three days. He has no idea. Would you make some promise to me so that I should get a divorce in order to marry you?"

He buried his toe in the pine needles, moss, and black soil. "It was my doing too."

She shook her head, face glistening. "It's my decision." She looked far into the distance, filled with hard calculations. "If he divorces me, I'll want something for my best years that I gave him. I can't let his lawyers trot you out and make me look like Downskate."

He stared at her dully. "I missed the boat somehow."

She shook her head, placed her fingertip on his lips. "No, don't. It's my life, my body, my decision. I made my decision to hold his cigar when you were still in grammar school. Shake yourself loose, moody swain." She spoke warmly to him amid her cold calculations.

"It hurts me," he said.

She drew him into the late shade inside a grove of mixed pines and wild-growing ferns. "What hurts—your guilt or your concern?"

He followed, towed along by his wrist. "I'm not sure."

Is this Jon plus Merile, or Merile minus Bill? It will always be a complex configuration, an intricate calculus, a kind of Three Body Problem, of orbital mechanics.

She embraced him tightly. Her wet face and warm lips ravaged his face. He felt the familiar stirring in his loins. He grasped her close, feeling the firmnesses of her breasts and hips against him. He pressed his hand, fingers spread as far as possible, over her buttocks so the material of her dress was slippery over the cleft between her buttocks. "I'm stuck to you like a magnet." He nuzzled her, choking in the warmth of her dry neck and shoulder.

She sank back with desire. "I need a quickie." She amended, seeing his expression, "We need a quickie."

Tears dazed her face, like raindrops spattering on the windshield of a speeding car. Her fingers brushed against his belt buckle. They melted back and down into a hidden little corner between wall and pines and heaped sand. She lifted her dress while he fumbled with his belt. Insects buzzed in their little haven and the sun came briefly out from the late summer haze, basking the air in a golden wine as they sought each other and found unity.

Chapter 21

Wondrous leaves crinkled in a late breeze, for it was the last week in September. Harvest is upon us, along with the full and singing moon. The Corn Mother begins her search again. She calls heartbrokenly about her on all sides—*peri-se-phonein*—while the Virgin Daughter once again becomes Queen in Hades, but the cycle is unending. She waits to be reborn under next summer's ripening sun, followed by yet another harvest. *Who now has not built himself a house, will never have one.* The solar system had swung past the jointures of equinox. The three-body problem rocked onward on dark, sparky tracks: taunting mortals with its mixture of oil and water, gasoline and fire, complexity and simplicity.

Andy had met a girl from the Paier Art School and now lavished embraces on her dark-haired, shapely presence. They seemed to be falling passionately in love. Andy had never looked happier, and Aurora with them.

Charles Egeny, resigned to memories of a summer fatuation with a married woman seven years and many tears his senior, busied himself transcribing memories of lost romance on his typewriter in the moth-filled garret.

Jon Harney still drove a taxi, conscious that Merile Doherty moved around the orbit of his immediate memory bearing a seed which might as well be ascribed to his feathering of her during the long and summer months.

This was the incept of autumn. A gray quality about the heat told him it was past the opportunity for summer love. He drove his cab in the poor parts of town, conscious of the loves and hates of strangers. Robberies and muggings were on the rise, and he resolved he would soon have to find another occupation. Meanwhile, women (strangers) he drove about offered him invitations to stolen love, sinister sex, secret *rendez-vous* or *rendez-fous*...

To all but one of these he said no.

To one such tender he did consent. Madrigal was South American, his own age, but mature beyond his years. She had run from some oppression and lived with a dozen family members in a house on the edge of Goatville. She was elegant and insisted he be gentle. She was divorced, she said. She had two children and her breasts were soft with milk, her nipples were loose, her hips bore stretch marks, and his taxi was her only means of escape from cloying, desperate, jealous, angry men in her family.

Madrigal took a taxi home once a week from her English lessons. She said she would feel safer, knowing him, so he agreed to wait each Monday night outside a certain elementary school. She was hungry for passion, and took him twice a week in the back seat atop East Rock Park—a common spot for rows of cars with steamed-up windows, including passenger sedans, the occasional taxi or upholstery van, and at times an airport limo. Madrigal was a small, lively woman with coal-black eyes. She was secretive and fervent, responding to his kisses with honesty. Her husband had stayed behind in their Andean city, evidently in charge of an *action grupa* of some rightist party she despised. Their whispered liaisons were quick, like snacks, but Madrigal was always thankful.

As a taxi driver, he was captain of a ship, and for some reason or for many and varied reasons, some women looked to him for solutions, refreshment, adoration, who knows what they sought in him. He avoided them all, stepping into the danger zone only with little Madrigal. He prayed there was no *Beel*, who would come with his *action grupa* and search for them amid so many vapor-clouded windows overlooking a sprawl of encrusted city lights.

At the end of September one day Jon Harney returned to his apartment and found a letter from New York. It was a simple letter from the firm of E. Eburgenhas, typed in halting Pica,

Please pick up your manuscript. Lovely stuff.
Have you published anywhere else? I'd like to
speak with you.

Chalmers

E. Eburgenhas

Irradiated, Jon pounded up the stairs to his room. The two Yale students had moved out, replaced by a Yale sophomore given to collecting butterflies and a Southern Connecticut State College student of teaching. The Yale student was hardly ever there, and the SCSC student was off playing folk guitar at some dive.

Jon Harney risked a few minutes at the typewriter, since it was after midnight, and Charles Egeny originated a brief poem. He reclined on his bed, dreaming of binderies and bookstores. He read and reread his letter a dozen times, each time gaining some added sense from its terse text. He fell asleep, while moths crept through the holes in the screen. He dreamed of Charles Egeny's brilliant future.

The next morning, he called the taxi company early. He said he was sick. He'd take a day off without pay—a sacrifice *por la causa*. Madrigal was already gone from his life, but he'd taken away a few words of Spanish.

Gray dawn had not yet turned into warm daylight as he had a breakfast of bacon and eggs to soothe his queasy stomach. He bought a bus ticket downtown, and waited for the big diesel machine in silver and glass to roll in on huge rubber tires. He dozed fitfully on the two-hour ride to New York City. For the second time that summer, he was *en route* to the pulsing dread-star—home planet and return to paradise sought by poets who wanted it all—Eve, apple, and tree with snake if only a typewriter and paper remained handy.

By ten thirty the bus rolled into the Port Authority. Despite air conditioning, Jon Harney was sweaty. Let this well be the last trip here. He did not care for New York City. Better to live casually amid the dogwoods and ferns of East Rock Park, where time had no meaning. As a cab driver, he confessor to the secrets of women. With Madrigal, he could exhaust the secrets of night. The distant city, in truth, could offer nothing more.

In New York City, he wandered amid tingling humanity. He was full of wonder today, and did not pause to wonder at anything more. Every street corner offered pretzels and buttocks in the shape of ice cream cones, but he did not stop. Clearly, the cryptic message from Eburgenhas was all that mattered. He considered dedicating his first book to the relaxed editors there.

"I'm sorry, Mr. Chalmers is not in," said the elderly woman tending the switchboard. There had been a sea change. The pretty young woman with violet eyes had vanished, or changed into this librarian of disapproval and gray looks. "If you are a writer, you are not allowed here without an appointment." She rifled through her calendar. "I have nothing blocked in for you."

Charles Egeny paused at the crossroad of his career. He said with sinking heart, "My manuscript is waiting for me."

"Oh really?" she said, while he fanned himself in the air-conditioned hallway. No nuns today. No old ladies in shorts. No young secretary in purple, with white teeth and violet eyes. The woman searched amid a pile on her desk. She extracted a manila envelope. "You are Mr. Egeny?"

He nodded, taking back the very same envelope he had brought one sweaty day in the early middle of a promising summer. He hastily opened it, finding his manuscript and clippings intact. After a brief search he located the note. It was a rejection slip printed on a common format. Underneath were penned the lines, "Sorry. Maybe another time. Power and beauty, but not for us. Better luck next time. C."

"Is that all?" breathed Charles Egeny.

The secretary regarded him with dismissive eyes.

"Is Mr. Chalmers in?" he asked.

She recited, "Mr. Chalmers is taking a two-week vacation. Can I take a note?"

He shook his head. "No thank you."

She pointed toward the door.

Drunk and smashed with shock and disappointment, he strode through the atmosphere of books and synthetic carpeting toward the elevator. It would be a long and heart-broken ride back to New Haven.

Was this karma, revenge, *Beel*, fickle finger of fate, greasy faculty conspirators whose reach had no limit? What had he done to deserve being stiffed like this? A cruel woman or jealous husband (or faculty colleague slash wolverine) could slash no deeper or closer to the heart.

The sweltering city outside bore a million possibilities. The eminent publication of Charles Egeny was sunk like the Titanic. He had been skewered by a casual and offhand rejection. Strangely, he was back at square zero, born again, fresh as a baby, diapered in endless draperies of possibility. Everything was once again as remote and intoxicating as a hopeless dream.

Evening descended with a clear blue brush stroke over the ocean skyline as the bus returned over the border from New York State into Connecticut. Sad white sails dipped on the Sound. Charles Egeny would start all over again. In that genesis, that hunt, anything was possible. He longed to return to his hot garret, carrying a case of beer under one arm, because an especially intense and poignant poem was making its lines felt under Charles Egeny's half-closed eyes as Jon Harney's gaunt, grieving features were reflected in the hard, cold bus window.

Cruel, senseless world.

Chapter 22

Wind murmured suspensefully, fresh as Creation. Dry, early leaves pressed up against the humming screen overlooking Merile's timeless porch.

Jon Harney lay in Merile's bed, feeling exhausted and feverish. Bill was gone, back to Australia. Merile, in her evening robe, brought a steaming bowl of tea and brushed his forehead tenderly. It was the week just when the cold front swept down from Arctic Canada, and leaves died by the gadzillion in bloody glowing lanterns and overflowing honey. In another week the sky would be leaden, and leaves just rustling husks blowing in circles on restless sidewalks.

Charles Egeny's heart died and was reborn in a bloodied and honeyed agony after his odyssey to the gatekeepers of mediocrity in the city that never weeps. His very soul intimed the arrival of autumn in a visceral, car crash sort of violent, stunned manner.

She bent her long, elegant face over him and he, wracked with the trauma of an early cold, looked with resignation and rebellion upon the young/old lines around her eyes and mouth. In the press and density of September, Charles Egeny had suddenly neared exhaustion and needed nourishment. Her warm, dry hand brushed lovingly over his forehead. He coughed rackingly and sat up in bed to accept the tangy steaming tea she brought from crocks and jars secrete.

"Poor Charles Egeny," she said softly. "All broken. I feel the same, so close to you. Drink, my poor love."

He ran a hand over the curve of her waist and hip. Under the night coat, her breasts hung willingly, offerings, near his cheek. Her thighs were smooth and rich to his touch. He coughed as he sat up to accept a steaming cup from her ministering hands.

She went back into the kitchen. He sat upright with his back to a pillow and wall. He cradled steaming cup and saucer amid twilight. Far away, a lonely carillon of bells from another century of Yale and New Haven clattered slowly and wistfully across evening air. The tune was Strawberry Fields by the Beatles. Its tentative, halting notes—much like a sweet woman's lisping whisper—seemed to say, *Nothing has changed. Why be upset? Time rolls on forever and ever. Nothing to be upset about. And look at us, we are here, together, in love. Nothing else matters.*

He felt smothered and loved in the aura of her caring. Bill had left, too quickly to consummate a divorce; the papers were pending in the hands of Westport lawyers.

Jon had a new feeling, finally, of belonging within the youngness and oldness of her apartment. His life was taking on that same timeless, experienced, tired resignation he heard in the caresses of that distant carillon. Those bells were there long before he was born, and they would be there long after he was gone; he and Merile and Bill and the hierophants of mediocrity in publishing and macadamia and all the rest.

What really matters? Love, probably, and only.

As he sipped his tea, he could not separate her wifeliness from her motherliness. It was a fatal dichotomy. He put the tea aside and stared with disquiet at the leaves blowing up against the screen window. No, he realized, he was not about to marry; it would all be a game of pretend until some reappearance of Bill or some other spectre of reality. In him, too, Charles Egeny—rogue and poet, mower of lawns, taxi captain and puffer at cigars—remonstrated at this all too easy passing of summer. He patted his stomach, pressing starchy sheets close, and reflected that she, like himself, had only just had a deflating trip to New York.

She'd gone from his life for a short while, during which she had visited a clinic in New York State and here Jon Harney's imagination shut down. He had not been consulted and she reassured him (as had Dawn and Andy) it was for the best. The child might have been his or Bill's. Nobody would ever be certain.

Marriage was so far beyond his horizon that it, too, was in the ethereal zone. He might marry her and there could be children. But when he was thirty (which seemed to him a very old age) she would be nearing forty. Charles Egeny cried out against this termination or smothering of the hunting and pecking instinct.

Merile finished her work in the kitchen. She returned smiling, with a tray of cookies.

"You smile like a calendar girl," he told her as she sat down on the bed.

Her blue eyes glistened. Her lips crinkled around white teeth. "That was so long ago," she whispered in a gentle voice, holding out her hand. She amended, "Could have been so long ago."

He took her hand and kissed it.

You are at the ripest point of all best things. You are beautiful with young skin and wise eyes. You are at your perfect moment.

Her lips were perfectly vulnerable when he moved close and captured her in his net. She rolled over like a cub when he played with her. They held each other a long time.

Chapter 23

Charles Egeny, alias Jon Harney, stood knee-deep in a pile of autumn leaves and improvised a swirling solo, punctuated by high, wheezing notes and basso comments while Merile clapped delightedly sitting on a bench under stripped, skeleton trees.

To emphasize his seriousness, he loosened his belt and let his pants drop down around his ankles. Thus he stood on the open hillside, echoing with leaves and trees, growling Coltrane-esque on an imaginary saxophone air horn, overlooking New Haven from the rusty cliffs of Indian Head Mountain.

He paused to look at Merile. She sat rapt on the chilly bench in that late brown-gold light, her hands folded child-like on her lap. Her narrow, fashion-model glowing face with sensuous lips and dark blue eyes was framed in golden hair. She patiently and delightedly noted his every gesture.

Seditious autumn air crawled like blood plasma around sweet-smelling tree trunks, raising essences of stored nuts and decaying leaves from around gray, knotted roots. Wind blew through his boxer shorts, and he abruptly let the saxophone evaporate from his open grasp. He bent to pull up his pants.

"Why can't we live forever?" he asked. The autumn forest could not answer, nor could she. Merile raised her thumbs in an Upskate, go-pilot gesture. She dropped her hands back into her lap, demurely, and glowed with smiles.

He offered a hand. She rose, and he led her along an old promenade amid strewn leaves.

"Jerry Lewis did that once, you know," he told her.

"Did what?" she asked calmly. As she walked, she regarded crumbling asphalt before her feet on the long-closed road. He found it strangely post-world, apocalyptic, this street that had once carried traffic. One day, when the human race ceased to exist, the whole world would be covered with dead roads like this.

She wore a newly bought olive-drab, military-looking ski parka. She'd thrust her hands in its pragmatic pockets, while her long brown skirt rustled around her softly muscled calves. She easily paced his sauntering stride.

"Stood in his underwear on a balcony in Manhattan and played the saxophone."

"Why did he do that?"

"To call attention to himself. It's how he started to become famous. Made the morning newspaper headlines."

She laughed. She tossed her head and her long blonde hair shimmered, imprisoned in her collar. "I'll never forget you back there, dropping your pants."

"My own brand of fame."

She extracted a hand from her parka pocket to twine her arm around his elbow. The smell of autumn was everywhere. It was a leafy smell, reminding of ink, of chlorine, of airy freshness.

She pressed a soft, warm hip against his muscular leg. "Someone will write a biography of you," she said.

He stopped, pulling her short. "When Charles Egeny wins prizes, it won't matter. No photos please." He rubbed noses with her as she looked modestly agreeable. "Except of you."

"Please, that's the last thing I need, a married woman having an affair."

They walked on. He stubbed through the leaves covering the road, uncovering with his toe a serpentine, barklessly smooth branch which he kicked sailing through the air. "This used to be a promenade during the 1890s. The road here was closed years later after rock slides."

Silently the regarded the motionless gray city below. Up on the parapets, he told her, above the stripped but complex tree crowns, were abandoned gun emplacements which had guarded the harbor in

Colonial times. Once as a boy, he'd found an unfinished arrowhead stuck in loam near here. He'd wanted to be an archeologist, but was kept from his goal by school and poetry.

He stopped and put his foot on a rock. "This reminds me of school."

"How's that?" She had put her hands in her pockets and was staring over the city, her face insular, her eyes probing far. She was about to tell him something. He sensed it coming and tried to talk and talk to stop her from saying whatever it was. Charles Egeny had been devastated. Now it was Jon Harney's turn.

"This smell in the air. We graduated from pencils to pens. Schoolgirls took to writing with laundry markers. They'd put their heads together over their homework and make big magic marker circles over their *i*'s. Teachers protested. Later came felt-tip pens. I preferred fountain pens. I made a lot of mistakes and has to erase often. You could buy an ink eradicator in a little bottle; it smelled like bleach and it turned the ink gold and then white on the page. That's what autumn smells like."

"It's a lovely smell," she said and inhaled deeply—a sigh from the heart. Her face was set and sad. "Bill and I will be moving at the end of the month."

"Where to?" Chills moved up and down his weakened legs. His breath caught short in his throat.

"He's returning from Australia. He'll have a teaching job in Vancouver, on the Canadian west coast."

Jon tried to recall his geography. "How far is that?" His heart already knew the answer.

Too far.

"Thousands of miles, Jon."

"We'll never see each other again."

"It's for the best."

"Anything is possible," he said bravely. "We'll find some way. Even if we have to make love in the snow."

She shook her head—*no*—but laughed and kissed him.

Chapter 24

He had a taste, during those early November weeks, before the return of William Doherty, of what married life could be like. With her, it was wonderful. Because it was a lovely golden doomed time, it was perfect. They both knew that nothing so perfect had happened to either before, nor ever again would happen. Her apartment was sunny and safe even though it might be raining and windy outside. At times the fall sun broke through, while smooth rock tunes warmed the air inside, like *Cherish* by The Association in 1966, an oldie just a decade later as time inexorably rushed on its Merritt Parkway of swirling leaves and anachronistic bridges.

Cherish is the word I use to describe all the feelings that I have inside for you...

She walked to work each morning through sifting leaves, and it seemed to him, watching from a window, that she hummed to herself with contentment. She'd stride away under stripped trees, among old Victorian houses, on her way to that office on St. Ronan Street amid gray, forlorn shades of coming winter. That's where they had met nearly a year ago.

He gave up his apartment on Edgerton Street to be near her, not to mention saving money he could spend on her. The proud black typewriter of Charles Egeny reposed on a sewing table in her living room on the street of owl-eyed windows.

This was a time longer and more perfect (superlative upon superlative) than their weekend marriage in a Rhode Island beach-front motel. Time stood still, and they shared perfection.

They made love long and searchingly every night. In the mornings, after she left for work, he would go for a long walk to prepare for a day's writing. Later, he'd put in a half shift at the taxi job, but his heart wasn't in it. He could not bring himself to face the future just yet, but after she and Bill left forever to land in far Vancouver, he would begin a new future for himself. He had no idea how or what. He might even leave New Haven, and start graduate school someplace. Anywhere other than New York City or Vancouver. Those avenues were closed.

He would go for a jog in gray dawn light. His shoes crushed through parchment leaves like a million discarded poems. Were any of them by Charles Egeny? Had any of them been thrown from the high stories of New York City skyscrapers, to flutter twirling down shafts of city canyon air? He had an image now of some goon who never read poetry standing at a high-up window while Charles Egeny's poems twirled in the air, and screaming in frustration for his money. It was all about money—nothing more, nothing less, and Jon Harney must earn his crust (and Charles Egeny's) by the sweat of his brow after the gates of paradise closed behind him forever.

As he ran, his breath steamed in chill morning air. He was reborn. He saw the world anew. He was at one with a milkman, a stray cat, a ten-year-old walking to school, a thick-jacketed woman raking leaves in chilly air. It was good to be alive.

That alone is worth the ticket to this crazy show.

Each day, he'd pick Merile up from work. They made a good husband and wife. They'd go out to eat, to a museum, to an art gallery, to a lecture about nematodes or papyri or codpieces. Anything is possible in a great university town. There were carillon bells to hear, organ concerts, violins, symphonies, jazz and rock concerts, Renaissance lutes, or warbling operatists. Especially poignant was a recital of ancient Ovid, accompanied by wistfully clanking kythara or melancholic soughing hydraulis or water organ. There was no end to magic. They would speed home and make passionate love as if each day was their last; which was close, because less than a month remained.

In November, while she was at work, he wandered into town searching deep stacks at used book stores. No Charles Egeny could be found here, only hope and pretense. Could Charles Egeny summon the passion again to compose fervent lyrics? Or had the assassins and vandals infesting Manhattan's money canyons destroyed his poetic epididymis?

He'd walk for hours on the city's streets and boulevards. He would sift impressions, filter memories, wondering what to take home with him to type out into reality. The days became shorter, leaves deeper, porch lights yellower. Each day, Merile would bring her special aura of patience and refreshing humor as Charles Egeny sat at his typewriter.

At any moment, she was ready for love, and wet, but she would sigh. He could have her any time, and he did often. Sometimes she would come behind him as he typed, and slide her hands into his pants and massage him to passion.

He gave up the pretense and took to sitting before a silently flickering television. Charles Egeny was hibernating or dead—no clarity on that yet.

As he became more frustrated, so did she. Not to mention that the midnight hour was drawing rapidly near.

* * * *

"No novel yet?" she asked one rainy afternoon as she came home from work.

"Dammit, no," he said, staring at a commercial. She left her raincoat by the door and stamped off into the kitchen.

He rose and followed her.

She moved tiredly, putting a pan on for mixed vegetables.

"I'm going to take a drive tonight," he said. "Andy Ferraro called. We're going to kick around some ideas about starting a business."

"Oh? That's nice." She moved about, dropping the empty vegetable pouch in the trash and stirring her near-boiling water. "What kind of business?"

He said, "Anything other than creative arts. Certainly not publishing. Maybe we'd manufacture lawn dwarves or something."

She laughed. "Oh my god. That I would like to see." It was clear she wouldn't.

He enthused, "No telling how far we could go. It doesn't matter what the product is. Books, lawn ornaments, poison arrows, calendars. Anything you can sell in a store that people will pay money for."

She stirred her vegetables, checking the quality of the gas underneath. "You're not doing much writing lately."

He said, "Merile, I try and try. It just isn't working."

She cast a dark glance in his direction, as if he were implying she was to blame.

He put his hands in his pockets and returned to the living room. Settling before the TV, he said "Thus, no cigar for you."

She came into the living room, slammed two plates on the table, and returned to the kitchen.

Minutes of silence later, he drifted into the kitchen to apologize. There, he noticed a slip of paper under a refrigerator magnet. On it was written *Bill* followed by a day, date, and time at JFK International on Long Island.

Part Four: Winter

Chapter 25

Andy," Jon said, "I wonder if you'd like to drive to California with me?" They sat in a cool back table area of the Kino Korner Bar. It being a weeknight, the bar was quiet and half-empty. A young bartendress hunched over her counter, washing out beer mugs with a face full of concentration. She seemed to shiver in her sweater against the cold seeping in. The radio was tuned to a local college station playing cool jazz from the 1950s. Radiators banged and sighed anciently in corners. A tousled Yale student in corduroy sat reading at a table with a beer bottle and ashtray filled with bent and twisted filters. Two lovelorn women held hands while they murmured in a far corner with their faces close.

Andy shook his head slowly and looked into his beer mug. "I don't see how or why."

"I thought you always wanted to see the far West," Jon said.

Andy squirmed. "Yes, but. Well, not now. I've got to save some money to go to grad school next year. I'm also in love with Yolica."

Jon rubbed himself on the cheeks. He combed fingers through wavy hair.

Andy looked up. "Say, you're not trying to run away, are you?"

"What do you mean?"

Andy toyed diplomatically with a match book. "Well look. I've been waiting for weeks to ever get a call from you."

"You've been busy with your girl."

"I know. She keeps asking to meet you."

"I'm about to have a lot of time on my hands."

"Oh." Andy looked sympathetic.

"Yeah. Merile and her lawn dwarf are moving to Far Gibrue out beyond where whales migrate and whatnot."

"Sorry to hear it. You haven't been the same since you met her."

"You haven't changed in the past year," Jon said in a voice freighted with irony.

Andy shrugged. "Dawn says the same thing."

"She's an authority."

"She is an objective observer. She's been worried about you getting shotgunned by the crazed husband."

"I slipped into a thing."

"Sideways," Andy said. "Head over heels. You have been out to lunch. I don't think you've even been to see your parents in a month. You're shacked up and lucked out over there. Maybe it's too cozy for you. Maybe you just need to get rid of the ballast. Are you doing any writing?"

Jon made a fist. "That's part of it. I can't seem to even look at a blank page without nausea anymore. Even the thought of grad school fills me with fright. I don't know what to do anymore!"

Andy cleared his throat carefully. "Say, uh, maybe you already know the answer and won't admit it."

"What do you mean?" Jon regarded him warily.

Andy gestured. "Well, uh,…you're getting laid regularly, aren't you? I mean, is there more to it? Or are you just so damn comfortable in your existence that you hate it, and her, and yourself?" Andy, having made his point, sat back.

Jon studied the whiteness of his curled knuckles. He said softly, "You've been my friend for many years." He stared at his knuckles. "I think you may be right." He looked up, feeling a strange mixture of fear, elation, and relief. "It's over now. She's leaving me."

"For her husband," he said with a twinkle in his eyes.

"I know. It's crazy. I'm being dumped by a married woman." When he thought of Merile, he felt as if someone had cut a hole in the sidewalk before him a million miles deep, and he was about to step into it and fall forever—a new meaning to *falling for her*. The thought of her in bed with him was possessive and obsessive. He felt a wrenching sense of loss. She was a drug he could not kick.

"C'mon, let's go for a walk," Andy suggested.

They walked under coldly bluish streetlights. Shadows danced where light fell between stripped branches. Rustling sidewalks seemed to roil with electricity as lights and shadows played nervously over the concrete.

Eternal night distantly echoed with highways and factories. It felt intimate but without compassion. In that clarity lay truth. Jon walked with his hands in his pockets and silent tears streaming down his cheeks.

Andy shuffled patiently along, blowing steam, patting him briefly on the back.

"Futz," Jon said as he wiped tears away and loved the night.

"Futz what?" Andy inquired.

Jon burst into a grin. "Just, futz. Aw, futz."

Andy nodded. "Yeah—what the futz." He added, "You're welcome to stay with me and Yolica for a while. You can sleep on the couch."

"Thanks. I think it may come to that."

"We'll leave a key under the mat for you."

They walked a long way. Andy puffed from exertion. Jon was thankful to him. Things had not turned out the way he'd thought. Distant highways murmured with tires, like a song or a suggestion, but he would not after all be running away. The solution was closer and more immediate.

A chill, soughing wind—aromatic with fallen leaves, irradiated with moonlight—was playful like an old friend. Dim gray house walls and scraping empty tree limbs portended infinite and rejuvenated liquid syllables and revelations for Charles Egeny.

"I think I'll go home and write a poem," he told Andy.

Instead, he took a long walk—to her apartment.

Chapter 26

Merile's apartment, when he arrived there at two in the morning, was in a shambles—very uncharacteristic of Merile. Stacked clothes, towels, books, utensils, were everywhere.

Fresh from his revelation, Jon clumped up the stairs and found Merile sitting on a suitcase in the middle of the living room, crying. She did not immediately see him.

He stayed in the doorway, hands in his jacket pockets, wondering where to start.

"What are you doing?" he finally said.

She looked up with red eyes.

He walked in and said, "You're picking him up at the airport?"

She nodded. "At ten. I have to leave at seven. I'm a wreck." She shook her head, blew her nose, and dried her tears, while he fetched two brimming glasses of iced tea.

"Thanks," she nodded, sniffling, as she accepted the tea. "I was crying because I didn't know if I'd see you again."

He sat down on the couch, hands folded peacefully and urgently between his knees. "How are we going to do this?"

"Do what?"

"Never see each other again. Live with him while I drive off to far cities and ports of call."

Renewed tears flowed from her eyes, and it wasn't the old contradictory Merile in that moment, taught to laugh and cry at the same time to drain her of all emotions. "I was going to let you have the apartment. The university wouldn't catch on for months."

"Thanks, but I would die here, knowing we made love and I could never have you again."

She nodded and sobbed.

"Do you want to do this? Go there with him?"

She shook her head.

He waited.

"I want everything to stay like it has been. We get along so well."

"Yes? And?" He stood with his arms apart, hands open, expecting a change of heart, some logic, anything.

She did not answer. Her stolid, distant look said, *It's a done deal—me and Bill, you and me—all of it was fate long ago decided and so we all move on.*

He watched her hands, and thought of holding them, but there was a barrier now. "I'm tearing myself apart inside over losing you."

She kneaded a couple of wet, wadded, ragged tissues in her fingers. Part of it was the shreds were hard to get a grip on, and part was she was so nervous. "Bill called from Hawai'i on his way here. He was crying. He wants to pack it all in and come back to me for real."

"And you?"

She stared at him with trapped eyes. "What else can I do? I was born and raised to be a powerful, wealthy man's calendar girl and hold his cigar."

"It's not a joke anymore," Jon said.

"It's for real," she said. She cried some more.

"You were going to move out and leave your apartment to me."

She nodded. "We leave for Vancouver straight from JFK. I won't be back." She cried unrestrainedly.

He sat beside her, took her in his arms, and found her stiff and cool toward him. She was no longer his. She no longer wanted him either. She belonged with Bill—holding his cigar in that commercial showing off his golf stroke, his hard smile and businesslike eyes, his winning fist on a cocked hip.

Don't mess with Bill.

She rose and paced away, with her arms folded defensively before her like a fortress rampart, off limits to him.

"I was going to pack everything and go to Australia."

"What?"

She nodded miserably. "I was going to beg him to take me back."

So that's how it is.

Charles Egeny sorrowfully patted Jon Harney on the back in a flickering old blue and black and gray movie.

She paced up and down. "But why? I sort of won, didn't I? He's coming back here."

Jon rose and rubbed his hands together briskly. "I'm going to grab my things."

"I already packed your bag for you. It's by the door," she said as if he were a taxi driver who'd come to collect her heart for a ride to the airport and then *finis.*

She put her iced tea aside and rose unsteadily. He suspected she had had a drink. She put her hands on his shoulders and he smelled a faint tang of gin, but she was entirely lucid. Her eyes glowed—a little sad, and deeply grateful in an entirely summary sort of way.

Are you going to hand me a dollar tip too?

Jon resolved to end this in a graceful way. He'd fall apart later, but that was then and this was now.

"Good luck."

She gave him an awkward hug. "You too, Jon Charles Egeny Harney. Write a lot of painful, passionate love poetry. You know I don't even read much." She eyed him compassionately. "It was swell. This was the most wonderful time of my life."

He touched her elbows but did not offer to embrace her. "I think it's for the best. Charles Egeny wasn't doing so well. Neither were you, I guess."

"I'll never need to have another affair. You've given me everything I'll ever need. I'll never forget you." She burst into tears and pressed her face against his chest. Her tears were hot and salty, as true tears of relief from anguish should be.

He embraced her, tasting her ocean salt on his own lips.

She pulled away, composed herself, sat on the couch. She blew her nose and wiped her eyes with a hankie.

Already, he stood at the door, holding his grip bag.

"Look," she said, "it's snowing outside."

"Oh geez." Sure enough, through the uncurtained windows, he saw thick gobs of snowflakes plummeting suddenly in the early hours of a blizzard.

"What?"

"I don't have snow tires on the Pontiac." He walked across the room and looked out a window overlooking the street in front. Cars outside were covered in several inches of virginal snow, which glittered under street lamps obscured by more flakes dropping like silent rocks.

"You're leaving?" she asked in a thin, high voice.

"What else am I going to do? We just split up."

"We didn't split up. We will love each other forever." She rose and glided close. She put her hands flat against his chest as if they were dancing. "Where will you stay?"

"With Andy and Yolica out in West Haven for a while until I get on my feet. Back to square one. At least I'm not moving back with mom and dad."

"Honey." She laid her cheek against him. "Please. Stay the night. I'll be driving to the airport. Three in the morning is not time to bust in on your friends."

"I can't. I have to get out of here." This was the past. He was ready for the future. Every moment he spent here, tearing away, was another rip in the fabric of his heart and soul. Time and fate were taking the book of Charles Egeny and ripping it apart, page by torn page, letting the papers flutter like confetti to the winds.

"I'll tell you what," she said. She patted him resolutely on the chest with one palm. "I have a rental car outside. It has excellent new tires that grip the road. I'll drive you to your friends' house on my way to the airport."

"Tonight?"

"Now," she said. "I'll get an early start. It's like oh-dark-thirty and half-past-late already."

Jon helped her carry a few things to the car. They dressed warmly. She made sure the gas was off, and everything shipshape before she locked the door and slipped the key under the mat on the upstairs landing.

Holding hands, they skipped down the stairs together, out the front door, down the snowy steps where sweet air like fresh bread filled their nostrils.

"You look so cute," he said. "I didn't know you looked so cute in mittens."

She smiled like a sixth-grader as she waggled her wheat-speckled knitted porpoise fin mittens before gripping the steering wheel. "I like to look cute for you, Jonny." She wore a knitted cap, the military ski jacket, corduroy pants, and suede boots with fake fur trip around the top.

She started the car and gripped the wheel.

"I don't think I've seen you drive before," he said. "It's kind of nice. I can kick back and watch you do the work."

"Watch me," she said. The tip of her tongue stuck out of one corner of her mouth as she turned the wheel. Looking all around, she navigated into the snowy street. "I won't scare you too much."

"I'm not scared at all," he said. He put his arm around her, and laid a hand on her thigh as she drove down the street. She headed toward State Street, and the entrance to I-95 that would take them toward West Haven. From there, she would take I-95 to the tangle of highways over the New York State line, and thence navigate over the bridges to land on Long Island for the final approach to JFK.

"You are making me wet," she said, and patted his hand lovingly with her thick woollen mitten.

Snow fell thickly as they crawled along I-95. Heavy fists of snow flew against the window. It was cold, dry snow. She had the windshield heater blowing, and the hot air kept the glass warm so that the snow melted as it hit. The windshield wipers worked steadily, beating a rhythm, left and right, pushing the white stuff out of the way. The rubber blades kept cutting wet, melting little splatters of water away to either side.

Not long after, they came to a familiar exit in West Haven. She sailed slowly and carefully down the ramp, curving around, to reach the wet, glistening street below. Snow plowing trucks had already made one pass here, and the street was lightly fuzzed over between tall banks of piled snow.

"You'll have to give me directions."

"Just go the way you're going."

"I want a nice kiss goodnight when I drop you off."

He said, "I'd take the ride for just one stolen kiss goodbye."

She smiled. "I was hoping you would care. Because I care. Charles Egeny—I want to be sure you're going to be all right."

He held held her slender waist in both hands. "One last time."

She seemed suddenly shy. "Really?"

He kissed her earlobe. In a short time, it would be over. He'd never see her again. It was best not to say anything out loud.

"You know," she said mysteriously. "I could use a quickie."

"Here in the car?"

She shook her head. "Too many snow plows and cops on the road. I'd hate to think someone would check on us to see if we're in trouble and find us, you know—*derelicto*."

"*In flagrante*," he said. "*Mucho erecto*."

"Look in the back seat."

"Huh?" He twisted around and pawed in the dark with both hands. "Suitcases. A pack."

"No pack. Open it."

He did. A sleeping bag popped out and unrolled. "Wow, that looks warm."

"It's down, made for mountain climbing. Nobody will notice if we duck behind the house for a short while, if we stay quiet."

"And you don't yell or moan," he said.

She laughed excitedly. "Just stuff my briefs in my mouth."

"We'll suck on them together," he said. "We'll salivate like two dogs pulling them apart."

"*Wow-wow-wow!*" she barked. Then she said very softly, "Touch me. Get me ready."

"After all—" he started to say. After all, they were still lovers until the last melancholy wink of red tail lights when she drove away on his street, and that would be the definitive end.

After all.

He touched her, and she let him, eagerly. He felt as though a hundred years of discarded history had just risen in a glad and merciful resurgence, begging binding like some final and overdue book of poems by Charles Egeny.

Le Fin au Début

Chapter 27

Jon Harney and Merile Doherty made love in the snow. The bluish light of the street lamps illumined spreading fans of glacial snow currying among suburban houses. His friends slept inside, blissfully unaware, as did the neighbors in their houses. This was a quiet suburban street where nothing much ever happened, aside from births, marriages, more births, and eventually deaths, in an ongoing cycle that had no beginning or end.

Together in her sleeping bag, they snuffled and giggled, moaned and cried together. He pounded her and she pulled him down for more. She bit his shoulder to stifle her cries. He shouted into her breasts before enjoying them with his mouth. She offered him her nipples and he sucked like a puppy while his hot dog relished her bun.

Afterward, they chased exhilarated over the snow fields.

They stashed her sleeping bag in the car. He fetched steaming coffees from a diner near the highway—the road that would now take Merile forever away to climes far out west, where the Pacific Ocean glowed long after dark with the setting sun; where Bill Doherty could teach and write about his discoveries in prehistory; where Merile could hold his cigar and look stunning at faculty parties.

Sipping gingerly at their hot coffees, they leaned on a railing near a factory-loading ramp. The world was coated white. Their whispers and giggles were muffled by the white coating.

"I hope you'll be happy together," he said tenderly.

"We'll make a go of it—a whole new start." She held her coffee as they stood shoulder to shoulder, looking over passing cars. One second you saw white headlights, then you saw red taillights, and then each car vanished forever, not to be seen again in his life.

Somehow, there must be no regrets. Only memories.

"I'll do the same here." He tried to stay upbeat. "That's life. A love affair, and we move on."

She shrugged, laughing. "Bill is still trying to shed his winter coat. That is, he isn't so sure of himself. That is something I discovered. Our problems won't be over in a heartbeat. That's why I wanted to exchange this little going-away present with you. To tell you how much I love you, I'll cherish you forever, and I'll never forget you."

"I will never forget you."

"I will try to help him. It will take time. He was hurt badly in Australia. Some broad named Lemony or Melancholy grabbed his cigar and ran away with it."

"Merile, while there is still time—I love you."

"Shush. I love you too. We shared so much."

Every moment, every gesture, was important. Jon and Merile stacked their Styrofoam cups steaming, buried them cup-in-cup in the intimate but merciless snow. Then they walked back arm in arm through the snowfields.

They walked back to the car. She drove to Andy's place. He'd sleep on the couch until something better came along.

Merile parked a block away, pointing the car at the highway entrance. "I'll walk you home," she said.

They walked arm in arm, trudging in the deepening snow. A plow rattled past. Its front blade scraped the street and threw walls of whiteness to the side.

Cars whispered on the distant highway. The night was filled with stars, with sounds of foghorns, with the familiar and loving sounds of a close and unencumbered wind. Her hair flew, rimed with frost. Her smile was white, her cheeks were red, and her eyes glowed as if she'd spent hours skiing.

"Are you going to make it?" Jon asked.

She squeezed his elbow. "Yes. I promise. Don't worry about me. And don't forget me. But move on."

They hugged long and hard. She cried again. He sobbed, touching her drippy blue lips. It was cold, but they hardly noticed.

They parted at the top of a rise.

After one final long, tender kiss, and a last failing grasp of two hands reaching for each other but pulling apart—she hurried off, leaving her lone, solitary track in the wasteland of snow.

He watched as she ran to the rental car.

He waved after her once more.

She was a tiny figure under a bluish streetlight.

He blew her a kiss.

She stood under that bluish streetlight, waving. She blew him a kiss from far away.

He waited until she got into the car and started its engine.

Moments later, she tooted the car's horn. Then, on sturdy snow tires, the rental car moved strongly away amid the feathery snowdrifts. All that remained of this love story begun on Saint Ronan Street was memory—a gold bracelet sunk in green water.

That's it.

The suburbs were quiet save for a distant humming of tires on the highway, wind sighing among sleepy suburban houses, and the forlorn, haunting muttering of foghorns on Long Island Sound.

She's gone.

1. About The Author

Jean-Thomas Cullen began publishing online in 1996 under the pseudonyms John T. Cullen and John Argo. More info at

www.johntcullen.com and www.clocktowerbooks.com.

As Jean-Thomas Cullen (his actual birth name), he has written the sentimental love story *Stop By*, as well as the trio of books dating to age 27: this novel (*On Saint Ronan Street*), plus his collection *Cymbalist Poems (1965-1977);* and *27duet*, which combines both books in one volume.

Under the **pseudonym John T. Cullen**, he has published a number of mainstream fiction books (novels) and at least one or two nonfiction books including *Dead Move: Kate Morgan and the Haunting Mystery of Coronado* based on a famous true crime and ghost story in 1892 Coronado near San Diego. He continues to publish nonfiction articles on subjects of interest to him, especially in History and the Sciences.

Jean-Thomas Cullen, a.k.a. Charles Egeny is shown at right at about age 20, circa 1970 while a student (and poseur) at the University of Connecticut, Storrs.

Under the **pseudonym John Argo**, he began publishing science fiction and suspense novels online in 1996. He was, in 1996, the first person in history to publish entire (not sample) proprietary (not public domain) novels online (not on portable media like CD-ROM) for reading online in HTML format. These works were offered in a then revolutionary new weekly serial chapter format 1996-1997, with the option to download the entire ms in TXT format. More info at the author and publisher websites.

For this trio, see www.27duet.com.

As John T. Cullen, he authored *The Spy's Daughter*, a sweeping and panoramic novel spanning the world from World War Two through the collapse of the Soviet Union in 1991. It's the story of a wealthy French countess who was adopted under mysterious circumstances as a tiny, abandoned orphan in a remote Siberian fishing village. She is raised amid wealth and power in Paris, married, with children. After a colorful and dissolute life, and the death of her playboy husband, she begins a global journey in search of her roots. She must find her enigmatic father, a U.S. Navy spy whose escapades covered three continents, involved atomic espionage, and incurred the ire of Joseph Stalin himself. Along the way, Tim Nordhall fell in love with a number of women and acquired at least two wives. But which of the women is Marianne Didier's real mother? That is a haunting and tragic story in itself.

Another John T. Cullen novel is the epic political thriller *CON2: Autumn of the Republic*, about a Second Constitutional Convention and its terrifying results for a shattered United States.

More recently, he has published a Progressive Thriller—a new sub-genre of meaningful political suspense fiction—titled *Valley of Seven Castles, a Luxembourg Thriller*. That is the first novel in which he reflects on his years of living in Europe to offer warnings about the present and hope for the future.

Readers can find most of his published titles on his three author pages at Amazon. Search on a name: Jean-Thomas Cullen, or John T. Cullen, or John Argo.

2. About The Publisher

Clocktower Books launched its pioneering, revolutionary online publishing program in 1996 (see *About the Author* above). We first published John Argo's suspense novel *Neon Blue* (today also titled *girl, unlocked*) at www.neonbluefiction.com and John Argo's SF novel *Heartbreaker* (in 1998 retitled *This Shoal of Space*) at www.thehauntedvillage.com.

By December 1996, we were launching an umbrella (omnibus) publishing operation called Clocktower Fiction, which morphed into Clocktower Books (www.clocktowerbooks.com) around 2002. You'll find more information at the Clocktower Books Museum pages at the website.

For a decade, starting 1998, we published the world's oldest professional online magazine of speculative fiction, *Deep Outside SFFH* (www.deepoutside.com), renamed *Far Sector SFFH* (www.farsector.com) in 2002. Much information can be found at the museum pages again; and we are developing resources at Wikipedia to capture some of this pioneering Internet publishing history. The magazine published both new as well as established SFFH authors, including nominees and winners of all major U.S. and international prizes including the Nebula, Hugo, Sturgeon, and others. In some instances, we discovered new, stellar talent. In other instances, we published a Nebula awardee (Pat York) and several top officials of the Science Fiction and Fantasy Writers of America (SFWA).

3. About This Book

The author tells us: "I wrote this novel in my mid-20s—in 2016 now some forty years ago. I'm not sure when or where I began it (New Haven, San Diego, K-Town), but its setting is New Haven in 1973. By the time I finished this novel in 1976, I had left New Haven in 1974 for San Diego; enlisted in the U.S. Army (1975), and was stationed in West Germany. During the writing in 1976, the story was already a marinade of nostalgia about a lost past in New Haven—a mosaic of life, love, & fantasy. As an unpublished manuscript—an excellent first draft cryptically titled *John + Merile*—traveled with me from one century into the next. By 2016, it's time to publish, at winter's door. A youthful, passionate love story never goes stale. In fact, I believe most of world literature consists of young love stories, for reasons I will elaborate at www.27duet.com and elsewhere. Reading this story, so many decades later, I find it almost another man's writing—fresh and new, like a 1970s disco album opened for the first time.

"At publication in 2016, I realized at the last moment that I should insert a few poems (for Charles Egeny, the fictional alter ego of the fictional Jon Harney) from my own poetry collection, republished in tandem with this novel because the two books seem like twins separated at birth and reunited many years later.

"This novel is very much the story I wrote at 27. I have polished it beyond the final keystrokes of 1976. Structurally it is virtually the same. The love story is what I wrote then. Polish comes from forty years of further living and experience.

"I was in 1976 already looking back on a rich life with many dramatic ups and downs. I'd earned a BA in English; worked as a summer interne newspaper reporter and student activist during college; hitch-hiked up & down, across the USA; was a published poet; had written several novels; spoke several languages; lived in several countries; already had a life by turns & twists of fate already wonderful, amazing, and terrifying. I was ready for more; which came indeed, by truck loads, as it does for all of us."

—JTC

San Diego, California

February 2016

Book 2: The Poems

Cymbalist Poems
Selected 1965-1977
by
Jean-Thomas Cullen

Clocktower Books
San Diego, California

Quote from introduction & dedication of 1980 collection **Pauses**:

"As we heard that cry,
And turned our eyes then
To the moon-drunk skies of Boston,
Knowing only that we were young,
And drunk,
And twenty,
And that the power of mighty poetry
Was within us,
And the glory of the great earth
Lay before us —
Because we were young and drunk and twenty
And could never die!" — Thomas Wolfe

* (*A Stone, A Leaf, A Door, Poems by Thomas Wolfe*, Selected and Arranged in Verse by John S. Barnes, Charles Scribner's Sons, New York, 1945)

Cymbalist Poems
Selected 1965-1977

Luxembourg

CONTENTS

Luxembourg

Book 2 Contents

Luxembourg. Unbearable.

NEW 2016 PREFACE: MY "27"

TWIN COMPANION BOOKS: This new preface introduces both my "27" collection of poetry (*Cymbalist Poems*) and my "27" novel (*On Saint Ronan Street*).

The term "27" started as an innocent handle in 2016 between me and my editor—an internal code, shorthand for my novel written at age 27. Coincidentally, twenty-seven is the mythological age when many brilliant young rock stars have died (a long list, from Jimi Hendrix and Janis Joplin and Jim Morrison to Amy Winehouse and many more). I didn't die, but stopped writing lyrical poetry and turned my lyricism into tilling rich soil for many prose novels that came after the "27."

These two books belong together as a pair of snapshots, like book ends, from a lost age in my life, long ago. I am just fully realizing this now—age 66, forty years later—near winter's door. In a moment, I will tell you the special, wonderful insight that made the intersection work and the connection click.

I can only summarize the wonder of this intersection for lack of space in this brief preface. I hope to provide more info soon at my personal writer website & canoodle www.sharpwriter.com. It's an interesting tale, and I am a story teller. The intersection of these two books became clear to me only in 2016. In 1980, I had published a collection of my favorite poems. By then I had also written and shelved the manuscript (Jon + Merile) of the amazing novel I am just now publishing forty years later. Only upon completing polish & revisions in

2016 did I begin to see how critically interlinked these two books really have been—both then (1976) and now (2016).

I stopped writing poetry around age 27.

(I had by then written several novels; I would consider my "27" to be my first really adult novel, although maybe today it would be a New Adult novel, written by a 27 year old reflecting back on a lost past life at age 23.)

I had been writing poetry most of my life, was a published poet by age 18, took away a Literature degree (English, German, Classics, History) at the University of Connecticut, and was able to type up a collection of several hundred poems by age 23. I salvaged those 400+ poems from a cardboard box into which I used to throw scraps of paper on which I wrote poems at all sorts of odd moments (restaurants, bars, guard jobs, you name it) over many years. I typed all the poems into a single volume while working as a security guard in the brutally industrial setting of a gas and power station in New Haven Harbor, and I still have that collection with me.

Readers of my "27" novel will be reminded of the author at various odd moments. Some of the romantic entanglements, drinking buddies, Victorian apartments, moths, typing, minimum wage jobs, neo-Gothic (faux, neo-Gothoid?) Ivy League buildings, and what not are all carved from the burl and grain of my real oak and life back then. A certain incessant playfulness of language is part of that special fertilizer the poet brings in nurturing sacks to the task of writing prose; sometimes too rich a mix; and certainly there is much in my "27" novel because I was still a working, thinking, emoting poet at the time.

The novel remained a dusty manuscript needing final edits over forty years, until today I am just finishing rewrites in February 2016 at age 66. The first marvel about this novel is how effective and poetic the novel has struck me and other early readers in 2016. It was a marvelous first draft, needing some polish, but virtually no restructuring at all (a miracle in itself). The second marvel is how it intersects with another major landmark of my year 27—the final and only collection of my youthful career as a poet.

I lived in Europe 1975-1980—working, traveling, enjoying myself while going through life's typical and sometimes not so typical ups and downs. I was stationed in West Germany as an enlistee in the U.S. Army, pretty much 9-5 except for duty and alerts, so I could put the uniform aside and travel anywhere on weekends and vacation days. My travels took me to Paris (often), and many other places including Luxembourg,

Frankfurt, Brussels, Berlin, Verdun, Speyer, Konstanz, an endless list of the known and less known.

* * * *

I should note that travel was always part of my life. I'd been born in West Germany in 1949, son of a U.S. Army sergeant major stationed in Nurnberg at the time, and an ex-pat mother who was a Luxembourg citizen living in Frankfurt after the war. So I was born a U.S. citizen, but lived my first ten years in various European countries as an army brat. English was my fourth language in life, after Luxemburgish, German, and a smattering of French. My first major pivot at age ten was when my father retired from the Army and we moved to his home city of New Haven, Connecticut. New Haven became my emotional map and experiential lexicon, filled as in anyone's life with both sad and glorious events. In short, New Haven (and more generally New England) were very writable for me. My family left Connecticut in 1972 to retire in the San Diego, California area, and I was to follow in 1974 after a few years spent as a starving artist around New Haven, writing poetry, working as a minimum wage security guard, and pursuing the female of the species (in equal measures probably). I should add the fourth thing, which is that I spent many an evening rambling around student and local bars around the city, drinking cheap beer and laughing raucously with certain cherished drinking pals. By 1973, as I say, I sat in the gas house typing my poetry collection, because I had a sense that I must do this or else they would be forever lost. I probably sensed that, in December 1974, I would pack all of my possessions (including the book of poetry, and a box of unpublished novels) into my old Pontiac and make an epic cross-country trip amid several howling blizzards to San Diego. I did not tarry there long (writing more stuff all the while) but enlisted in the U.S. Army. I was simply not ready to settle down, and I wanted to see Europe again after an epochal absence, and that was the easiest way to accomplish the trip.

* * * *

That is how I ended up in Europe 1975-1980. Forty years ago as of this date—February 2016, which itself will be ancient history soon enough; time to get this show on the road, better late than never—I was a young U.S. enlisted soldier stationed in West Germany. I had the good fortune to miss the tragedy of Vietnam, which ended two days after I enlisted, and to be stationed at a relatively cushy office job in Kaiserslautern. My war was the Cold War, whose realities were with us every day, but underscored to me on a tour of Berlin in 1976.

I served two enlistments there. All of the material here concerns my first enlistment, which was in retrospect the assignment of a lifetime, a dream, to be stationed in Europe, working 9-5 M-F except the usual Army rigmarole, but otherwise free at a moment's notice to drop everything and spend a weekend in Paris, Brussels, Luxembourg, Berlin, Frankfurt, or a thousand other interesting places.

At the same time, I spent many an evening and many hours continuing my life's writing career. By age 27, I already had a poetry writing career behind me or virtually over by then. In 1980, I selected my favorites from among all those poems, and self-published the selection as Pauses: 64 Poems (Copyright © 1980 by John T. Cullen, All Rights Reserved). The publisher (yours truly) was Fresh Press, Kaiserslautern and San Diego. I visited a German printer at the time, bought some supplies, and on his instructions created a primitive case-bound set of no more than a dozen copies, of which I still have a few on hand.

At the same age (27) when I stopped writing poetry, I wrote this glorious, ecstatic, symphonic love story whose manuscript title remained simply Jon + Merile for forty years until 2016, when I am now finally publishing it.

The novel—now titled *On Saint Ronan Street*—was a nostalgic, almost deliriously sad, gloriously emotional and sensual romp into a past that was simultaneously real and imagined, truth and mythological, autobiographical and fictional.

The hero is a young (23) college graduate named Jon Harney with a phantom-limb English degree, limitless energy, a minimum wage job, and an idealistic passion to become a famous poet. He falls into a hopeless but lyrical and wonderful love affair with a beautiful young married woman named Merile. Her husband is a professor of archeology at Yale University, but is always absent without emotional leave. At the moment, Bill (her husband) is on a dig in remote Australia, and digging all sorts of extramarital chicks in Sydney. In fact, he calls her to say he wants a divorce, before he calls her to say he doesn't. Merile is understandably alone, up in the air, and just in time for a wild, crazy, breathless tumble with the Poet. You get the connection.

Here's my flash of insight, which completed the connection between novel and selection.

I was finishing the edits on *On Saint Ronan Street* just this week (late February 2016; updated 1 May) and it occurred to me that throughout the novel, I have Jon Harney (under his pseudonym as the alleged Russian émigré poet Charles Egeny) claiming that he is a passionate and aspiring poet, but how do I show that?

I realized that I should sprinkle a small selection of Jean-Thomas Cullen's poems (from Cymbalist Poems) into the text of the novel. I promised to tell you the special, wonderful insight that made the intersection work and the connection click. That's it—I put some real poems into the novel, and I am telling you about the novel here in my larger poetry collection. One day, I will probably make available some more of those old poems from a lost age.

What this does for me is amazing, in my view. It rescues my poems from ignominious (agnominious?) obscurity. At the same time, it adds tremendous juice to the batteries of one Charles Egeny, a.k.a. Jon Harney, a.k.a. yours truly (mythologically sort of). Call it validation. In this grandiose stroke, I was thus able to complete the circuit and close the connection between my to "27" books.

At my website www.27duet.com, I will add more information for lack of room in this brief preface. The title *27duet* is of the book containing both the novel and poems under one cover—also available soon in print and e-book editions.

**Companion Volume ("27" Novel—On Saint Ronan Street)
Matches this Poetry Volume**

(See the New 2016 Preface about My "27")

INTRODUCTION 2014

Note: This introduction dates to an earlier edition of the poems, before they were integrated into the "27" trio that includes the author's novel, poems, and the 27duet (combined).

The poet spent a chaotic post-World War 2 childhood in Luxembourg and other European countries as the son of a U.S. Army service member and a European mother. His mindset was devoutly ritualistic (Catholic), yet blissfully free-thinking, at least as early as age eight. Of those incense-wreathed and stained glass hours only a fragment of earliest poetry survives. Ironically, the city is only about 75 miles from Arthur Rimbaud's childhood drama in Charleville-Mézières, Ardennes, France.

As an adolescent in Connecticut, Jean-Thomas Cullen (a.k.a. John T. Cullen) attended the R.C. high school of Notre Dame, West Haven—but wrote in a secular style that preserved the pieties and fervor of the earlier while painting freely the world as it presented itself.

The high period came during a fragmented post-Beat college presence (or absence in all but body). Alternately haunting coffee shops and book stores, when not hitchhiking among the concrete pillars and cold lights of a clockless time, he wrote of women and discoveries, empires and memories real or imagined. He belonged to no school except the jazz itself that pattered strongly in his mind and blood. The poems speak for themselves—that is why they are poems.

One week in his early 20s, while working as a security guard at an industrial cathedral in New Haven Harbor, he brought in a typewriter and a cardboard box full of scribblings, and—amid the industrial steam and savagery of this old haven—committed hundreds of penned or penciled scraps (napkins, cards, school paper) to a typed journal in between clock rounds where hummocks of dirty ice lay over frozen gravel. He carried this bound thesis with him on a solitary drive to California, and then on a flight over gilded, rosy clouds to Europe.

Five years later, in his late 20s, he wrote the last few poems while stationed far off in West Germany during the Cold War. He had written several novels by then, and folded his entire sheet of music into the prose that occasioned his hours by a cold gray barracks window, listening to Mozart in the autumn river of his blood.

At that time, he selected what he felt were the best of his best, and published them in a small, hand-bound volume titled Pauses. A third of a century (over half a lifetime) later, he made a similar pass through, and selected the same poems again—he had been right in 1980 about his choices. From undine memory, he even corrected a few adolescent syllables to move back to precisely where they had originally been written, so that was right too.

See also: *Notes*, at rear.

LUXEMBOURG
(c1956)

Making faces.

1. Wir Ehren Dich
(fragment)

Iesus, wir ehren dich
Fur jeden Lanzenstich.
Mit deinem Blut und deinen Schmertzen
Hast du reingewaschen unsere Herzen...

Age 7, Luxembourg

WEST HAVEN

(1960s)

2. Saturday Feast In Little Poland

I watch each Saturday in Little Poland
at Allen's Peerless Junk.

It's a ghoulish feast (before lunch)
of licking, lapping flames,
small bodies in the open pit.

They crouch upon a vast
glittering fallen Goliath with
his armor and his baubles -

(You can almost see the giant limbs
outstretched,
   a hand upon a sodden chest,
   and think of that
   sausage jumping
   in the bubbling pan at home) -

Chewing little rubber, paper, oilcloth islands
and cardboard cliffs
with rippling, snapping jaws,
but seeming to devour little. ⇨

Black, smelly smoke whirls upward,
hot within a cold aseptic wind
    Etching in summer
inky filth on a humid sky;
    In autumn,
dark warmth in cold gray air;
    In winter
disappearing into streams of falling snow
that cover the lukewarm scrap heap with
a grayish film;
    In spring
Green:
testimony to the new by old things burning.
    That's all year round at Allen's Peerless Junk
on Pilsudski Street
near the black old iron railway bridge.
    So come, won't you,
come with me, our bellies empty,
and we'll watch the flames this Saturday
(thinking of bubbling kielbasa)
feasting before their week-long fast.

ND 1964/65

3. Alien

Velvet currents, silver bubbles
in the deep
below an amber water sky...
!To stand on a pearl dust planet
A million miles below a certain
                    bobbing bow...
Alone
Among a billion fleeting shapes,
    Alien,-
    (darting silver daggers
       gaping rusty discs
         hacksaw wings...)
    Here is death a quiet dream
    (barracuda fins
       puffs of red dark
         devil teeth gleaming through)
    the end of nothing.
Alien, I!
among the shards of Eden!

ND 1964/5?

4. Autumn River

Swirling roundly, river flow,
by cobbled banks
and marshy shores,
racing like the clouds
in the cold grey wind;
Standing windblown in the eddies
at your swollen rim,
reeds and swamp grass lean,
beaten by the spray of
foam boats rolling by;
Running moody, River talk
to fish laid on the banks, and
wild geese darting in the gray…
Under wharves and bridges, 'round
small boats backing as
you roll along; ⇨

Gripping frothy waves with
curling fingers ride
dying leaves, drifting
from the marsh stream in a circle
then into your center stream;
Dark waters, run along,
with your booty on your heaving back,
squawking as you rumble, but faintly
for the noise you make:
Festive turkeys stolen from the farm,
bucking boxes from the pier, and
trees you've bitten off with
grinding teeth of thunder;
Happy am I, with
my net ashore, and
my dinghy on the wharf, and
my pantry filled for winter feasts:
Godspeed, Autumn River!

1965/6 ND

5. Interplay

Green expanse,
shimmering glass
    roof.
    Wind there is,
water runs
    nowhere.
    Glimpses:
Cherub face
    vanished in water;
    Age-green watery metal fixtures:
Victorian cherub, youth,
green with age, what is this vision?
    Trees, over the flat roofs away,
green and young beyond wetness
    in wind.
    Cherubs: trumpeting memories,
Nautilus shells filled
    with tomb ash   and yet
        green leaves
    scrubbed and dripping
    in cleansing wind!

ND 1966? Rooftop/study hall 3fl
over gym *or* some Yale college?

6. Luxembourg

On a table standing in the grass —
Victorian bones of wood clashing with
    spider blades -
Rests the sky rocking softly
  as the ever lightly haze
   brought forth from tremors of vastness
   echoes from an empty hall filled with
 silent wind
  and colors.
   Wind
behind my eyes
fills my forehead with hair
waxes my cheeks
dries my lips
   From the village where the people live
the church bell is ringing noon:
   Wafting sensations of stew, of sauce, of
meat, unstoppered wine, sense of
  being somewhere else or nowhere
(hunger) but how possibly in this place?
   The hay, the hay, Jean Pierre
The tails off the carrots, quick!
Come, children, we shall pray;
Eat, for it is given;
yes, the fields

ND66/67?

7. Sand And Sun

When
a dog ambles across
scathing sand with wagging tail
head bowed before the booming breakers
turning clumsily on four legs to
catch the brilliant sun, full on
a friendly canine face
pale tongue
    when old weary legs lie stretched from
a wall worn by sand and wind
feet encased in old black lace-ups
feet tired
and sun makes tired and wine makes tired
and eyes make tired
    Sleep
    Sleep - grit has lost its teeth
wind is like warm water -
warm
tingling mixture
barking happily

ND67ish?

8. Ancient Poets

What do the cracked poetries,
the broken rumblings and mumblings
fleshy buttered lips of Catullus,
windy time streets of Ovidean evenstill,
    tell ME,
who gaze at the crescent moon
dipping its scimitar sail
on the wind-blue sea
of the beautiful city
        city of towers
        city of showers
        brief and sun-flecked,
        city of white ramps and bone arches
        whose immensity spells breathless? ⇨

     (Catullus—
your sparrow never looks up,
hassling breadcrumbs
earned sweat-drenched on the latifundia,
in the microcosm courtyard;
in these walls
grasses indefinite as Gallic rain:
Here is every blade, indeed, a blade of grass.)
     (Ovid—
I dream of
golden apples
& fleeting white limbs   tinged with
borrowed shades of light)
   Still, the alleys are blue bone,
though you are
both so many centuries still now, quiet,
I only wish I could ask you questions
about life and love.

NHJC summer 1967/8?

STORRS

(1968-1972)[1]

9. Sees Itself

conch of consciousness:
two-edged *
　flitting sea-scissor,
　sword of existence *
　in the dread shallows:
　　That * instant
(round the wall)
retreat *
　And sees itself.

?Storrs 1967/8?

&
60¢
steno success
    open
spring door
Coca Cola
/
skirt
  hi,
**(see p.
    dominant and.
stocks bru bra
broke the
!
typo'
bond paper
desk calendar
    "Coffee with)
    open door
Spring
voices
"While I
    a fly!
want to close
the door please?

Musics #3/Spr68/Davenport

11. Composition I

on a white wall:
switches, three:
OFF, ON, ON

Musics #10/Spr68/Davenport

12. West Haven

there was some minor civilization already
when still only oystermen dredged the green
Sound:
    tucked-away deep and warmer breeding
places;
sea-weathered piers; small gray houses;
where desperate shrubs in dark green armor
eat the aggregate cliffs, and in the tidal marsh:
    cold wind picks his way between tall reeds,
turtles crawl, salt water grinds
  half-finished arrow-heads

                  coons prowl, owls howl,
                        ⇨

Winter dots the beach
with ice puddings, Spring pebbles the sand
with snails commuting on the tides,
Summer: Oil, sharks, jelly fish, and the
mating ritual of August king crabs by night,
Autumn: driftwood
     and on Ocean Avenue, under the trees,
  chestnuts,
  ankle tide of sifting leaves,
over the pavement wind by day, moon by night,
pumpkins, overturned boats, dark football
imitations of war

                                          1970?

13. Your Eyes (Ennui)

Your eyes are not on fire;
you sit with lyre in lap
leaning against the window
    where evening's sun nectars
deepen, making you drunker;
    My eyes chance to caress
your white thighs, soft breast,
    your belly all tawny
and honeyed in that opiate light.
    Your-eyes are lustrous,
half-closed;
No there is nothing to exchange
more reddish than glances;
    And so will you remain,
lazy and reclining between
amber curtains, panes of glass.

1970?

14. Hot Dog Vendor On The Beach

The wealth was in the hot dog vendor's hands:
Timmie   had big round blue eyes
     bought two   ate his
       gave one to little Janie who
       broke hers
       gave part to   ate hers
              Spotty the dog-
       and so there were three.

McM?1970

15. Jazz Trumpeter

Jazz Trumpeter at climax of a
particularly demanding solo:

Heow!

(lips to the horn,

puts his lips to the horn)

Heow!

Camus 1970 Spring

16. The Wish

As it always will,
summer rain reminds
of autumn thoughtfulness.
Sudden chill, darkness,
uneasy wind in the leaves,
the unease mere melodrama…
because all is and was as
it was and always will be -
Man, and the Wish to Be.

Unk Storrs 1970ish

17. Rediscoveries

That
which discovered long ago
smells good, again and again
That which rediscovered
after once found
long ago and with
ooh and aahh
never loses
its power to surprise
again and again
What was once given
is given again
and again,
coming in disguises
or at a different hour,
on a different train maybe,
but this fresh
ever market
again and again,
Morning,
or Spring sunshine
or a new Love,
it feels so good again,
and never lose the
pebble to enchant!

?Storrs 1970ish?

18. Sun Worship/empire

We worship the Sun.
Even in our architectural criminalities
    is justice, as in the dagger's shining eye.
        All light is the light of atoms and stars.
        The moon and the knife
share splendor's distance.
The knife is on the Earth's dark side
— stabs but she does not whimper —
and the knife is
    miles, miles from the Sun,
    miles from the Moon.
        The Moon is an eerie dream of the Earth head.
The knife is carried by a lunatic messenger,
    who built the pyramids,
        drowsing tortoise herd in the desert.
        In the Sun.
        But the Sun also shines
on the archaic sky line of New York.
        The winds there
(the windows are opera glasses)
    sing songs of empire.

McM70Spr

19. Affirmation

Welcome, World, with all your vinegar!
Welcome, Reality, triumphant beast!
Welcome, Sunlight, feast of splendor!
    After the deep galaxies of my brainself
are done exploding
And the abrupt, calamitous young stars
   finished with their wild music
    Welcome, subtle golden sunlight
who sting my narrowed eyes,
and ride the sweet summer wind in the
leaves, green airport of insects!
    There is, after all, only one fate,
one destiny, bereft of gods and devils,
free of angels, demons, deaf to prayers,
mysterious to squinting diviners. ⇨

This is my destiny, limited but honored credit,
to take upon my shoulders if I chose —
   and choose I do,
like Bunyan wrapping the ox around his neck.
I want to carry my fate beyond the fence
toward the looming green-black forest
beyond the symphony of my best years.
   As the dull black cipher
unfolds into a mighty dream,
so there is, again and again, only morning
to drive the night away: Precise,
rich in changing colors,
vibrant and harmonious guitar,
the well-tuned life.
   All things, from here, follow of themselves:
Dawn the night which follows day,
insight the dull cipher,
perfect mnemosyne the splendid here and now!

Storrs?1970ish?

20. The World Not Right

The world was never right,
I guess
    In the good old days
the devil was loose
roaming the world
seeking the ruin of souls
    one awoke at night
sweating in dread
at the howl of a dog
chained to a fence
at the edge of town
edge of the world
    where men have set foot
on the moon
was an alien planet
thought to be a face
made of cheese,
with unknown terrors, tygers,
behind fitful running clouds, ⇨

    where today
against the sweet silver moon
runs a gleaming 707
easily surmounting
the dark turquoise sky
    We who huddled in caves, cold,
afraid even of warming fire
poured from the sky by our
generous sky father/earth mother,
    afraid we were, afraid we are,
still all the old instincts,
still that sweating in the night,
world not right, never right,
poor world, poor us.

Storrs 1970ish

21. New Haven

East Rock: Cannon eyes overlooking the city
with its sea; its forests and rivers.

Indian Head: Old gun emplacements,
  where a stick to the hillside
will turn the loam, expose bones and
arrow heads damp with seasons;

Old stone bridge & winding 1890 promenade
& rock slides & abandoned road.

::::600 years after Leif: Wood ships on the
Connecticut River, landing at the red light
near College Street and Frontage Road;
settlement; prayer; wharves, warehouses;

::::in the 1600s a ghost ship was seen
foundering
in a stormy night. Fires were lit on the rocks
and boats set into the brine bristling with
boat hooks but ship and storm and night passed,
by day men returned sculling under sour clouds.
Days later the ghost ship
upside down and under full sail   crossed in a
rainbow several times by Morris Cove. ⇨

::::Turn of the century: Morocco; Long Wharf;
Smedley's warehouse; where horses shipt raw
from the West were broken by Nutmeg cowboys.
::::Connecticut River changed course. The
ancient
bed is now Exit One, Downtown, where Hooker
knelt
End pray'd, wellspring of I-91, super highway,
whose glass/metal waves roll into foggy Vermont.
Today
on the overpass,
smog fishes   with beak
   and lays new eggs.

1970

22. Lavender Express

Lavender express, hear me in your dignity:
I abuse time, am buffeted (and your shoulder
   is hard as the next) but none my fault.
Take then my bitter tendrils, my roots, shoots,
my herbal corona, unbury me from the wires;
I have stopped, and am ready to start over.

1970?

23. Pear Picking Season
(fragment)

at random, a luxury:
hands in the fence, shaking
clustered leaves, gnarly twigs
as glistening sticky
globes dangle
then drop
plop plop
one by one.

Coventry Fall 1970

24. For Companie

Fingers smelling of wood swarths,
like bacon from the fireplace,
She kept me Companie;
    In the room in the cottage,
in that roome by the lake,
she kept me Companie;
    Round-breasted, rumpled white sweater
stuck with bits of autumn leaf,
alive with borrowed fire colors*
      (* and we catalog the burning of
fires, and homeliest
is wood burning in fire places,
food in iron places,
bacon and chestnuts, wood
and auburn hair, such a girl was she)
    Her hair, her sweater, warm, emanent
with fragrance of fresh leaf
and common burning wood: Wine
from Madeira, Virginian tabacos,
were shipt to us,
for Companie!

Coventry winter70

25. Coldfall

I see
whirling autumn leaves
a turning clock
    I see
turning autumn leaves
a whirling clock
    Night has fallen
the cold is come
    a batting of the
eyes —
not more
    a pointing finger in
a window vibrating with frost:
Night is come
the cold has fallen
    Nibbling nights with fresh-bread breath
fumbling figures standing in snow
darkness has come
darkness has fallen
    the cold

?Storrs or NH 1970ish?w?

26. Spring Fever

(fragment)

Softly visits the gurgle-bird,
spring gently presses,
  heartbeats quicken in
  the quilted hay-yield,
Spring gently presses.

Camus 2.19.71

27. Race

I became conscious of your race
    briefly
confronted by your spread thighs
your sun-yellow curls.
    I am dark-haired,
descendant of Kelts and Saxons;
  You
   of Angles~ Farthest Thule.
    When I saw your moon-white curls
thought of your fairness soured
  (briefly, precious vessel)
    I remembered your snow-haired warriors
whom my people fought.

71?Camus

28. Courtly Love

The words are spoken from our fingertips:
    Love, you are best to be with.

You are swift in piercing, hunter—
    my heart seeks you everywhere.

    Pictures, portraits,
    lutes, and pergaments;
White stag bleeding on the rocks;
Two lances broken in his side.

Spring1971

29. Shipper

stately sailing captain of the line,
he sh'd'f s'd he borrowed night from night,
blacker breath than icy coal barge,
and flecked, by star, wif beer spots.

Turns he, Dane/bearded and sez:
"Harum," - this by way of pipe tar sediment -
"Alter's outen Afta by bright bell Scorpion."

:::sell me no stick to stir yr mire, ape, I,
I travel on the wave tables,
I log the ice floes under Comae.

Ferial night - shiver; boreal; aureal;
crawl, whight, to your tree and see
what siren combs stir my so pocketable waves.

Storrs/Camus? Fall/Winter 71/72?

30. Nocturne

Your wind, my empty friend,
come to fill my open hands —
the night is his bellyful purse,
come to clatter pennies on my knuckles.
   The mountains in the city have neon.
   A trumpet is still, I know, because
because of his hand, to her breast,
and her hand, rising to caress.
   An empty coat's the wind's tent,
air in trumpet's wet with osculations,
he signed his name and
folded the canvas away.
   Somewhere, I think, butterflies
   and children.
   Gomez saw and heard the elevation.
Eddie cried and sang and drank
   into his radio.
I am a stranger here
but these streets treat me
as if I'd never been away.

                              8/9/71 3 a.m.

31. Indian Summer

Summer is Indian).
the weather is mild
September is the last
Indian, I guess
Like any of us
Mild,
and Conquered.

Coventry, 1971, Fall

32. College Youth Ago

That gone ecstasy, that madness under the
       hill's lip.
Homer's ships tried these shores in vain.
Sails furled, silence made them
       drift away.
The beer cans sank before dawn.
Pink dawn: Dinosaur buildings
       frozen in mist.

1971?

33. Flight Line

In this tangled life maybe,
one touch of beauty,
or a hint of the Great Love,
for the much so indistinct,
the sky, this is surely planet love;
    I want to hook
     into you
     my sky line
and give you gas
so you turn gold and groan:
Hey_____

    Which is, after all,
the reward,
the hook-up, the sky flight,
my love to yours, you
who I am not.

1971?

NEW HAVEN

(1971-1975)

34. Night City Clarion

— ?where were you, she, warm, says.
— !I was, I say, crawling in the girders,
  the night city.
    Head open, friendly February,
Mild flavors of Spring night, intimations
cleaned of nicotine & able to savor the
    (cocktail music used to clean blue ring
  bouillon dish
  in burnt-ash dust-carpet old doorman
  hotel-) air.
    February, febris, feverary, early fever,
And all that old ragtime face,
leaning out with the shredded wall ads,
from the doorway,
    The Town, Old, covered always with
yesterdays
and yesterday's words, her ads,
  her thought balloons.
    Mannequins, my ballet,
  downtown , the empty streets,
  friendly lovers promenade, steak
  and violins, old wine, cellophane,
  wrap the windy streets in fog sheets.
    Foggy night, cat steps,
eyes in the fishbowl, rondeau,
MY MIND IS SO PAST IDEOLOGY!
    In fog, invasion fleet: cadillacs,
  minesweeper gowns, gents with
    carnation semaphore,
To the opera! And where, really, succeed?
    (I just don't know,
  not too strongly, I, ⇨

I just don't know,
   not strongly at all.
      Sky rain: Tinkle as it falls,
early warning: pull in the newspapers,
the News is pulled to safety,
only strong as the paper it's printed on.
      Alto sax.
Tiffany bubbles.
Tap room—closed.
      No new mythologies
—disbelief is sleep—
old-myths-sag-in-fog.
      Cadillacs, for the Easter visit, early:
In the fond night, dreams of spring.
Innocents, we, phantoms of the old new faith,
nets we are to gather airy alphabets.
      Alone, along the fog streets,
tripping only on ultimate acids
of the body trip;
      Roll out the Puto,
and Haul up the Sum! ⇨

Not heartless at all, but no longer feeling
cold, nor darkness, nor the city, or people,
nor messages, nor saxophones.
   In the city,
 In the city,
 In the night city,
 and. phantoms in every chrome elbow.
   Flowers, Flowers for the city —
bring Brussels, Paris, Berlin,
Rome, Vienna, and London:
all the dreams, memories, the museum,
stacked here, the curator is
blundering old Jonny Tundaboid,
75¢ expert whose fingers and lips
probe cracked sidewalks
looking for, not his, nor Clark Kent's,
but old Dream King's footprints.
   I circle, oblivious of history,
waiting for Spring (papers in the rain)
wheels out on the blind air,
waiting for the landing light.
   Waiting for the words to dissolve
like salt on my cheeks, the rain.
   Open, City:
Open, receive the rain:
   Your flowers,
last blown kisses,
as you sail from your harbor.

                                 Feb71New Haven?

35. Samba Of Shade

agua e umbras - this I drink, from your shade,
oak trees, the very sun is chlorophyl green,
the wind is warm, moist, wrapping itself
like the juice of ripe, thick leaves
around my hungry pores.
The mysterious bird's throat
is the secret Eleusynian well
and a mirror to   quaint water gurgles.
In a turban of opiate heat
I release my swollen head to alight in tall reeds.
There, black mud weighs
The black mud among my footsteps
weighs my impositions on Maat's scale
balanced by tall reeds.
The self, the will, are in the clouds,
harmless, evanescent, my thoughts like bees.
Evenings are wind-drawn
in the mature organic processes of my thoughts.
Swallows, arriving north for Spring,
have, in truth, no mind for precedent.

Spring72Schiavone's

36. Christmas

That fresh drizzly foggy night
it was Mona and me
and Henry brought the tree.
    Mona and me
(we are ever innocent
of our so many tomorrows)
and Henry heisted a tree.
    To the warm house
we brought the tree.
It was too big and
I drove with the top down.
    To get it through the door
we had to cut it in half.
    There was just too much,
everything too much,
in that little place, good nook,
we drank our beer and passed
the hours, Mona and me,
    Later making love
  (after Henry went home alone)
under the tree.

NH 1971Xmas

37. Lost Love

(icy moment)
Ruthlessness has no cuttinger edge
    than a love reconspired alone
    and cut from itself
    in the ice
Of rediscovered solitude.

Schiavone's Spring 72 PostBP

38. Island Story

The dull oak by its trembling leaves
dreams the acorns' bounding gonadity.
Drunk on sunlight, we climb the mast.
We scan, tattered, for passing virgins.
The horizon, however, has shrunk;
all is but a dream, a prayer,
the reenactment is a resignation.
A strong, narrow-eyed youth climbed the oak.
He saw the ship and sailed.
Later as a young man he fell captive to love
in a Berber queendom. A vengeant king
soon came and slew the youth.
Ever after, a quiet man with troubled eyes
paces the island's tropic rim.
With binoculars he scans the mainland.
The youth's grave is but
a shallow plot of turned earth
and the leaves shake, rattling, over it,
the man visits it often.
The king's spear lies gross and green
in the ocean rim.
Sea horses dance in the boiling waters,
conches sleep on the deep highways;
No virgin waves in the misty distance.

3-20-73 G&H

39. Seaman's Farewell

Men recently emerged from the sea
tend to sunshine, vanilla, and soft company
Men who have swum ashore
like to head home in late afternoon
carrying striped bags, ice cream cones.
Men
leaving their armor, their halberds,
pitards in steaming salty sand,
like to dry themselves before the screen doors
of shops dry and scoured inside
like the gleaming chestnut she11
redolent chic cork, leather, polished driftwood.
⇨

But come time, they back against the sea,
arms spread to the stone cliffs.
   Silently, reluctantly, they take their armor
   from the sand,
   wrap themselves in drying cords
   and belts
   of moss-green sea weed,
   pick up their king crab shells and
   barnacle-and-scallop crusted tridents,
      and walk slowly
      into the deepening tide.
   When cars are parked and naked knees cooling
                  under kitchen tables,
The sun drifts to rest
among tangled trees.
   A buoy abandoned on a sand bar
comes to life with the tide.
   The waves of the sea are briefly bowls to the
sky.
   The closing of the waves
Over the last wave of a limp hand
is the merciful end to a lingering goodbye.

Spr72/postBP

40. Piano

My thoughts played piano
long and softly from your eyes.
I could have put your apples in a jar
but there were places to stay
(while you chafed to go)
and you left
(you said you would)
me in poetic triumph

1971or2?

41. Lost Love

(timeless moment)

The hearth is visible.
You, fine girl, broke the flowers
which became running greyhounds
at the wetted fireplace.

?72NH/postBP?

42. Singles Bar

Are you going early, and alone?
Stay. We
are the driftwood of
conversation, fragments of
ambitions, broken halves,
the late lamp. In this
our deep and distant eyes
glanced to agree.
Stay. My voice
is inaudible, but my eyes
Are screaming.

G&H late 72

43. Dogging Her

...Dogging her: we are all Indians.

Early cold whispering into wood confessionals
respells morbid and groping presexuality.

Far cities (cold nights,
stale beer, intimation French fries,
gurgling wharf walks) fresh air:
New Haven, New Haven, Port Nouveau,
reenactment, resignation:

All potential resolved
combination by combination
by pairing, intersection, erasure,
short circuit, to the one final
bumper stop. Stop. ⇨

Realizing mortality is the first true gesture,
the last spontaneous action: We are dogs
ambling in alleys of time
Caught in the autumn and evening
before spring and day are satisfied.
    …Dogging her:
O thee, O thou, we dog her heels,
and she is mortal (dagger, oh truth!)
if and only if
to the autumn mind,
rusty leaf, snow flake, compass,
crucifix, structure and coembodied purpose,
rimed ice, black iron hinges,
cage
of minutes, days, and hours.
    Oh and she has blonde hair-fall,
milk skin stippled pink by cold's seduction,
blue and guiltless eyes.
    Her body is perfect,
statuary,
we dog her heels,
she too is only human,
we devour her shattered condescension.

?New Haven/72ish

44. Cafe Macho 1

Man of great deeds, o violent life!
He sees his story as one of drink and smoke:
precipitous, with red nights and lightning days;
painful encounters with careless or impulsive
women;
friends with guns - he is of battlements,
   sailing ships, and cannonades!
     Women (when they see him lingering
         with his Marlboro
         over an expensive drink)
think: there
sits a gentle and unsuccessful man.

New Haven 1972ish

45. Cafe Macho 2

Your string has fallen,
pharaonic dancing girl,
I see your tan skin
in the flute music;
in the liquor,
the dusky lounge,
the airconditioned dance place
with women to pick from,
pastiche of loves
that might have been
were it not for...
What tender celebration
if you were you
and I were I
but here we are all
the should be,
the would be, and may be... ⇨

She walks out to accept this dance,
her eyes are black and fierce,
her beauty is terrible, ringing,
like an army with banners flying.
    She deigns to accept this embrace
from the ninety-ninth shadow
of the man she gave her soul.
    O essential grace,
the jazz of your dry skin
is beige and angled in motions.
    You evoke, essential grace,
music; it was I, once,
who took your soul.
    For the space of a dance,
the embrace of a trance,
quite by chance,
we relive my long ago night
and some evening of yours
    before you had your hair cut and styled,
when you possessed your youngest beauty.
    Your smile is a white feather
floating in my air-conditioned eyeballs.
    Your tan and tennis face
is full of invitations,
reasons, address cards.

                                    ?New Haven 1972ish

46. Refrigerator

Paired Towers of Health:
a quart of orange juice
a quart of milk -
beaded with cold droplets -
On a hot summer afternoon.

Unk?NH1972ish/reflOrangeSt1962ish

47. Birthday

(fragment)

I begin to feel
measureless loss of youth -
itself
abdication from jeweled childhood.

NH Canner Street 1972 Fall

48. New Haven Harbor

Your death, broken horse, on the iron tracks,
defines the meaning of the Sun;
The nature of your blood, the Moon.
Your torn brown hide, leather already,
says that something happened
                which is now past.
Something is now past.

?NH Harbor 1973?

49. Moving In

This is a stark place.
The room is empty and the night cold,
   autumn chill smells of leaves,
   the only light is that of the moon
on a hard polished wooden floor.
   the music is a vagary of tentative
piano notes from some other existence,
some other apartment of
neighbors not yet known.
   Sing to me softly, radio,
devoted presence which
hull us both against the cold. ⇨

This is a stark place,
a new place, an inbetween place.
Much is left behind but of
the new world there is nothing yet,
only gleaming promise on
moonlit wooden floor, .
hinted smells of wax and paint
    and autumn leaves,
    unaffected piano notes
    unaware of my intruding ear.
    Sing to me, softly,
envelop me, hull us,
for this moving,
dread moving, the nothing new
and nothing old, the autumn cold,
all things had to be left behind,
and this is a stark place.

?Piano Music prob MrsBurgey's Hamden73/4

50. Everscenes: Silver Surfer

Memorex MacOedipus, to an Older Woman
(while sating on music, beer, snow,
                and pork shoulder)
    Self calls, future,
free myself: your
cloying musky fingernail love,
cruel and malignant unselfsufficiency,
big scared wet black eyes,
panic reaction, cage of frenzy,
parsimony of time,
salty electrolysis my own crumbling teeth…
    Wham, Bam, Thank you Ma'am,
durling, yes, I AM the Silver Surfer,
shoot between the stars,
a hairless gleaming oscar; ⇨

        I am the award, the reward,
rider on the silver board,
shoot between the stars,
pound your unpopulated beach,
rock against your trampoline;
your reaching eyes,
your encaverned thoughts seek my
        flying form.
        Yearning
from the head of your Albert and Victoria
steams around my silver torso.
        I am in the transporter room,
younger than you, my bald silver head
glows in your round animal eyes — my, baby,
streamlined godlike face.
        I could be lost in you,
silver needle, jet, arrow plane in
        your late sun,
Daedalus I am you melt my wings,
yours are thunder and lightning. ⇨

I am dawn, man, immortal, and you
　　　　　the dying dusk.
I will not lie in your arms, die by
　　　　　your charms;
you move me, you BEHOOVE me,
Ulysses dazed and oil-drenched in
　　　　　Circe's bed, wed,
but I, yes, AM the Silver Surfer,
sky master, cloud skipper,
I surf above your bleeding earth
touched by the welcoming warmth
　　　　　rasped by tigress claws…
　　　A dozen arrows pierce my shining legs,
　　　　　my beautiful legs;
as I fly away silvery, hard, youthful
　　　　　and without mercy,
I am stained with the lingering golden
　　　　　afterglow
of your broken heart.

New Haven 1974

Fort Ord - 1975 (Basic Training)

KAISERSLAUTERN

(1975-1980)

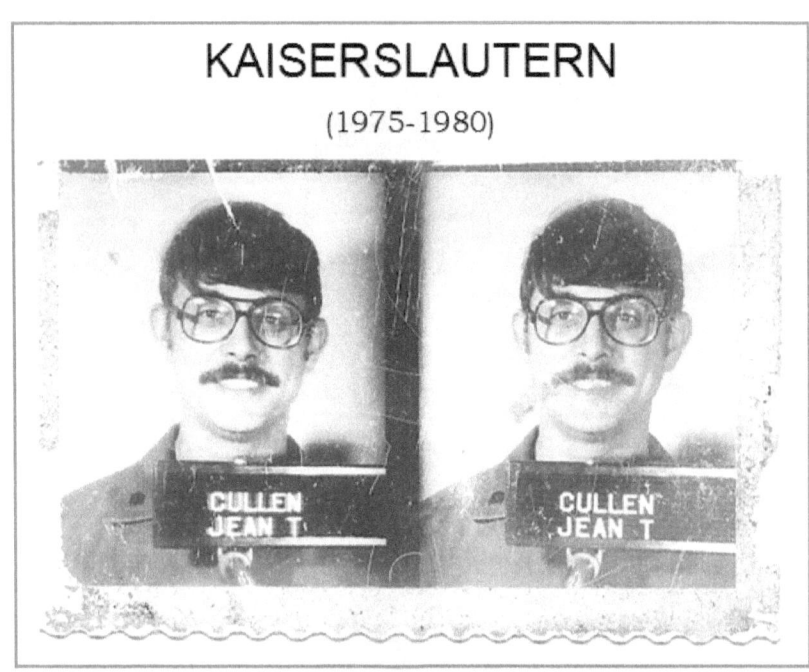

51. Elan

Afra-Shemuth: The cat made syllables
pouting its undulating hackles
by the mahogany chair leg.
   The rug, where she practiced her claws,
burnt if you ran a finger over it.
   Coffee was made
and betrayed
my need to escape.
   Tobacco was made to glow,
shimmering blue smoke wreaths
in the motionless air: I despaired
                  of escape:
                  Turned traitor
            to my moment,
            to my hours,
waited, burning in tobacco, didn't want
to meet her parents.   Read old
glossy magazines slick with ad promise: ⇨

Afra-Shemuth: The ad man
bought clay, blue at Stonehenge,
powdered the rich Canadian birches,
smeared Penna charcoal into ink,
bought glossies, Apollo resplendant,
the ad man laid the message
on the mahogany table top, wreathed
    in shimmering blue smoke wreaths:
    Afra-Shemuth: The Pomade
of Stutz owners, Harvard Pendant,
on White Field, Gloved Hands at the
Wrist Couped, Letter H, Gules...
    Afra-Shemuth: Unkempt but fair?
Afra-Shemuth: Seeks affair?
    Don't despair.
Rub it in your hair.
It's the bear grease with flair.

Unk Late/KTown?

52. Some Late Hour

Loneliness is trumpets. Fire in loins.
Silence is music, the creeping time.
I need to embrace but no one is here.
T know no sweet soul lost in mine,
no arms and eyes warmly reach for me.

I am alone in a foreign land,
in a city others hold dear since childhood.

That I left my own dear city
means my soul is hot and dry, a
fevered thing yearning for water.

Home is far, far, on the day side of the world
and all the unseen whistling jets
are going there tonight.

No one can embrace the moon or the stars;
their warmth is shed elsewhere.

No one can bear the silence or the fire,
the trumpets, the music, heat in belly,
and soul like baking stones.

No one can ask time, no one speaks with
silence, no one can be happy alone.

Ktown 1975ish?

53. Army And Air Force In Southern Germany

Autumn leaf sunlight:
here in the forest
where some Roman maniple may have rested,
evening cookery, where the seasons
are as epic yet.

Willowy Cardumnii women walked with
water pots
and later the rosy, beaked Germanii.
Here. This well of retrospection,
this eternal mud, foggy winter, bronchitis,
while our pine-imprisoned armor sinks rusting
into the slide and slag of brown hillsides.

Here, Mars, Pallas, your arrows poised,
celebrate your curly-haired rebellion, have done!
Those Druids will speak no more,
The pearl-handled colts are Excalibur, sunk
in stone.

The Sun, red head, swims in the frosty jet
streams,
Thunder whispers. On the dew, water droplets.
Boom, an omen, Hymen, o Hymenaie, marriage
of moon and lightning, Bangsalot,
campfire tale, and then Cardumnii slumber,
Keltic sleep.
Sleep, Midnight, sleep, Warrior babies,
golden heads and blue eyes, pink wet lips,
until you wake again, gaunt missiles.
Above the transparent storm,
on blue funnels,
spring larks wheel in spirals.

KTOWN 1975/6

54. Spring Sunlight

(fragment)

Sunlight: You spear of introspection,
              dream of love,
          You long inhalation
            and sigh of time!

55. Paris

(cities eternal)
In cities eternal,
bright fires are fed
with moth-like people who come,
and dance, and vanish.
Paris, like Rome like San Francisco,
endless pageant, soya feelings
and paper discoveries, soul sponge,
timeless, immortal, when we
are so achingly mortal.
Go Friend leave the City;
find the individuum
away from these words and smiles;
some rotting home sweet home
on a festering river
where you've known every fishing spot,
every place to go parking,
every corner drugstore,
every season, all your life. ⇨

Go to the place
where you first found love.
    That wine
was sweeter.
That memory
is dearer.
    There is no love among strangers,
no home among monuments,
no sleep under foreign gables.
    Go to the place
where you walked with your eyes closed,
where you can die remembered,
where you can live among old friends,
Home, where you came from,
the Only.

UNK/NHorKTown/Dr.Mormile said c1971ish

56. Homage To A Nude

O Cheek and Smile,
ye buttock moon,
orchestra of fingers,
long legs, and pink belly,
pear breasts with stem nipples,
center fold, still life,
still I think it is the
source of light—
your smile.

KTown 1975/6Playboy Ctfld on wall

57. Mid-Point For Odysseus

Where, steady plumb, beaded eye
is mid-point for Odysseus?

    He, guileful Danaean, after leaving Circe
and all the ogres of other-destiny,
asks again: Ye dis, is it shore I see,
Penelope's house, where the
long-tongued suitors pant, and, yea,
  she spins?

    Spins — unmindful, straight-eyed,
sure of this truth against all others,
the inherent destiny, the fate itself
Odysseus could not see
for her, for him, she spins the cloth,
her wheel is a machine of sparks and stars.

    Is it I, he cries, staggering
  from the wine-dark sea,
   dripping and heavy on the pebbled beach,
I, who thought too much?

    Is it I who went too far, only to return,
who come alone and disguised
this late hour, this late day?

    Where, steady plumb, beaded eye,
is mid-point for Odysseus?

KTown 1975/6

264

58. German Girl On A Train Near Homburg

Heidebron (Meadow Fountain): sweet blue
eyes,
yellow hair, Frisian smile, Kiel, where, I imagine,
God's drum pounds on the North Sea
and the seething water foams open
under ice and sun
to emit trumpets of Arctic poetry.
A flame burns in the ice.
Your brief nearness taught me an hour of Mozart.
Sea water, briny and smelling of fish,
is decorously sipped in those parlors.
Ladies wear fur and growl in the streets.
O Hanseatic angel, breath of sagas,
your tartan smeared with candle wax
from the night's dancing — ⇨

Slender ship, farewell, back to your North.
Like any pale young queen who worship-
ped wooden pantheons under moss and wood,
you have drunk eagerly the blond wines
our gods give us down here in the south.
Briefly you furled your sail,
touched your flying breast against Paris,
sought in the warm and turbulent southern lands
the same vineyards and monasteries sacked by
  snow-haired warriors long ago
and now, laden with treasure,
you will return to the beer-like sea,
the bear woods, the palinged outposts,
the high German music, Hamburch,
  burhuc.
    So long, dear spirit,
kindling message, bright fire,
sky eyes, snow hair, sun smile,
meadow fountain, sweet eagle,
forest partridge, smiling, farewell!

KTown 1975/6

59. Oriole Flight

Your oriole flight is
apprehended;
You fall, banded,
land on rooftops,
tar gums yr feathers.
Inca, Inca, your dreams
are memory, your journey
is ended, your wings
Are broken
(never was
nor ever will be).

?KTown 1975ish?

60. Twilight

As light is slowly extinguished
and deep peaceful sleep settles
are all good children home by the fire?
As the night comes,
ragged field of gnawing stars,
heart-breaking stretches of eternity,
are you a close and loving family?
As the immense earth turns and groans
in the stopless bath of solar music,
are you alive and alone and in touch?
Are you in the parade?
Is there not some glow behind your
dark windows, some warm spirit
nosing about the gray old walls? ⇨

Before the cold earth takes you down
again to the worms and their merry friends,
is there maybe a dance you'd like to hear,
a song you'd maybe you and me
and just the smiling vinyl orchestra?
Should we think of homeless children
and John Astor suffering from crepititis
or drag a stupid dog sopping from the rain?
Yes, and light a pipe
or maybe type;
  Sing at the piano, foam a beer,
  steam the windows with good cheer
Before we pull up the white sheet
careful, regretful in the darkness,
and slide into our cold bed?
Yes, and only the music,
sweet smiling-music,
as daily each new Columbus
discovers this fertile harbor!

?KTown 1975/6ish?

61. Tesamon's Testimony

Time is testimony from simple Tesamon
who died upon Priam's field.
He gave to his wife as she did to him
the time due one another.
What truly captured him
was her love.
They gave to one another time,
and time alone is what is valuable
in this short life.
Those two, they gave each other
their youth, a treasure none may take back.
When he saw she loved him
He melted inwardly,
treasured her gift, for
once, she was beautiful,
and he never forgot
how she offered her young years.
Somehow, no greater sacrifice
was ever made.

KTown 1975/6

62. Tesamon's Mother

Sing, simple Tesamon, the baby you were,
the delight you found in life.

The sun's warm rising dispelled the night
so often, when you cried for milk.

Your mother was rich, and gave breast
offering coos when you cried.

Never forget that kind hand which raised you
and those loving words in the dear kitchen.

Like mother, like sun.

Her rays streamed over you, irradiating you,
and the wealth she gave you made you a man.

The anguish of your death under pointed
sword
was only your mother's, not yours.
Life was full, because she loved.

KTown 1975/6

63. God Of Buildings And Trees

Underlying the shapes: geometry and poetry
and the good life is a taut guitar,
its strings measured, then bent
by the roaring ocean of perception
    The fight with random agglutination
proceeds and a given flower
should be picked from this rushing car
    How easy it must be
to read the truth, the way,
and the life from a book
    More exciting to wrestle with angels
and love the Lord still as I love me
when I love you loving me o music
and poem, flashing dance, architecture!
    Under the words is the ocean
in the ocean are the fishes and
among the fishes are sharks
and glowing things ⇨

Where the birds are is the
wild fresh air without order
unless you know the whole
and then, still, the
pro and causa recede infinitely
because there is only so much time
and hormone excitement to play with
all the different clouds
      On a meadow in time
are the graves
I visit them
when my piano is alive, electric,
and the good loves are there, my
flesh and. blood and memory -
do you deny me this, God of the Law,
when you made it so?
      Do you take my tears of joy
as a prayer when I have good music,
do you maybe
sing and tap along with me, Lord,
when I have found good rhythm
and love all the whole wide world?
      Are you happy when I am happy,
when I sing I would be born again
and again if I could I would if I could
again in your world and
the lumen of your numen
is a blaze in my whole this way?

KTown 1975/6

64. Moth

You annoyance,
— brief —
because after a moment's anger
I reflect on the justice
    of your presumption,
      the dignity of your proclamation,
as you enter your last wild dance,
— dervish —
moments before you die thrashing
in the cauldron of desire
around the light bulb.

KTown PanzerKas 1975/6

Photo: San Diego, about 1985,
Jean-Thomas Cullen & Carolyn.

Ending Notes

The dating of the poems is essentially from the typing, in 1974, in New Haven Harbor. For each poem, as I tried to reconstruct its context, sometimes years later, I inserted my best guess as to when and where I wrote it. In many cases, the info was written on, or decipherable from, the original scraps of paper. In other cases, I added my best recollection during the compilation of either 1974 or 1980. In this final edition of 2013, memory is too faint to register, so I am at the mercy of my younger self nearly half a century ago. That poet was at last as on beat as I am today, if not more so. I am surprised to find an uncanny memory-ear for a precise turn of phrase, the right syllable in the right breath, or just the right punctuation *here*, not *there*.

ND stands for Notre Dame West Haven, my high school. UConn stands for University of Connecticut, Storrs, place of my undergraduate studies in English (with relateds in Classics, History, and German). Homer's ships could have been Homer's blue bicycles (1968 Mr. Babbidge bought 100 for all to use, with destructive results). NHJC stands for *New Haven Journal-Courier*, the extinct morning side to *The New Haven Register*. One poem, I think, on a remarkable late afternoon, overlooking briefly sunny rooftops after a rain, as a luminous blue dusk just as quickly grew. Camus was our existentialist monicker for The Campus Restaurant, a now thankfully extinct greasy spoon filled with rotten food, watery coffee, and shady characters. Coventry and Ashford (Hashford) are two Connecticut towns were I lived off campus from UConn for short times. KTown is G.I.-speak for Kaiserslautern, Germany. Mrs. Burgey was an elderly landlady.

Dr. Mormile was a mentor during my early 20s, father of my dear friend (sadly as of 2010 also late) Jim. He had a PhD from Yale (1930ish?), in Romance and Classical Languages. He served with the U.S. Army C.I.C. during WW2, and then made a career with the CIA in Rome. He retired to his home city of New Haven around 1967, and taught part-time at Quinnipiac (then College). Despite his love of Rome, and intimate knowledge of its topology, he told me one homey Thanksgiving Dinner that one should live in a small home place where people are not transient souls as in great cities (Rome, New York, London, Paris, and the like) but are rooted in time and place. It was a magnanimous but melancholic observation, filled with nuance, that I would ever treasure.

(JTC—San Diego, January 2014)